EVERY GOOD PLAN

A CHRISTIAN SUSPENSE NOVEL

URCELIA TEIXEIRA

EVERY GOOD PLAN

AN ADAM CROSS CHRISTIAN SUSPENSE

URCELIA TEIXEIRA

Copyrighted material
Ebook © ISBN: 978-0-6398434-7-6
Paperback © ISBN: 978-0-6398434-8-3
Independently Published by Urcelia Teixeira
First edition
Urcelia Teixeira
Wiltshire, UK

www.urcelia.com
books@urcelia.com

To my three boys, Noah, Micah and Elijah,
who without, none of this would make any sense!

Your encouragement, support, and hugs when I needed
it most are what got me through the long writing sprints.
You have my heart!

"Many are the plans in the mind of a man, but it is the purpose of the Lord that will stand."
Proverbs 19:21
(NIV)

CHAPTER ONE

F or the first time in his life he felt fear. True fear. The kind of fear that drains your body of every other emotion and then spits you out to rot. The kind that penetrates the deepest, darkest corners of your soul and has you suddenly question the purpose of life. A life he didn't know was even worth fighting for. It would have been so easy to give up. He no longer felt pain. He no longer felt anything. This was it. This was how he was going to die. Death suddenly felt far more exciting than ever before. Almost welcoming.

As another fist slammed into his already pummeled jaw he snickered inwardly. He had found himself in many tricky situations over the forty-four years of his miserable life, but this one took the cake. This time he had somehow gotten himself caught in a snare he didn't know how to escape from. And unlike all the other times he had come close to situations like these, he had always managed to talk himself out of it. Not this time though. This time his greed had finally caught up with him.

Perhaps his little sister was right all along. He was a good-for-nothing idiot who'd had this day coming. She'd certainly predicted it plenty of times. But she was too young to understand why he had chosen the life he had. It wasn't as if he ever really had a choice in the matter anyway. He had his father to thank for that. Now there was no turning back. His luck had finally run out. Luck, as if that really existed. His life had never been one filled with good fortune or success. He took whatever scraps had come his way and did what any other cursed sod would have done; survived.

Another blow to his nose interrupted his wretched thoughts. It yielded him nearly unconscious on the ground. His body pushed down hard onto his already broken arm. That was the first bout of punishment they had served him. But he had felt that type of abuse many times before. An experience that had made it easier. A bolt of pain shot up his broken limb as if to emphasize the memories he had worked so hard to forget. He wasn't numb after all.

In the distance he heard the command come to finish him off and suddenly he was faced with a decision. Should he give up or should he fight to live? But before he could answer his question the decision was made for him and he felt the sharp edge of a knife slam into his back. He counted four more thrusts before Lucky Lenny blacked out.

IT WAS DEEP INTO THE NIGHT WHEN THE SHRILL SOUND of a passing car's horn brought him back to consciousness. The sound of several more cars rushed past him, their headlights blinding what little vision he had left. As his mind tried to piece things together, he realized he was still lying with his face in the dirt, his broken arm pinned beneath his mutilated body. He drew in a few shallow breaths. His ribs made a cracking sound in his ears. Again a feeling of self-satisfaction came over him. It seemed neither he nor his attackers had any say in whether or not he should live. Something or someone else had had the final say. They had certainly given it their best shot at killing him. Left him for dead somewhere in a ditch on the side of the road. But they had failed. He had survived... again. But somehow his survival was different this time. He could sense it. Instinctively he knew that Lady Luck had nothing to do with it either. Then who did? Who decided he should live?

He managed to lift his head enough to see he was only about twenty yards away from the road. A road he didn't recognize. They had pulled a hood over his head before they threw him in the trunk of the car but if he had the chance, he'd wager on being at least an hour outside Atlanta. Another set of headlights pierced his retinas. Obscured by the shadows of a nearby tree and the pitch darkness of the night, he would likely not be noticed at all. If he could somehow crawl to the edge of the road, he would at least have a chance of being spotted by a passing vehicle. It was worth a shot. It was his only shot. The only one he had right now, considering his unfortunate predicament. He tried moving his right leg up to push his body through the dirt but couldn't. It didn't respond at all. They must have damaged the nerves in his back when they stabbed him. Instinctively he tried moving his left foot and felt the sweet sensation of pain from the sharp gravel under his bare toes. Relieved to have feeling in his left leg he pulled his knee in a forty-five-degree angle next to his weakened body. With his right arm broken and still pinned beneath his frame, he stretched out his left arm, digging his fingers into the gritty soil. He drew in another few short breaths before he pushed the side of his big toe down into the ground and tucked his fingernails firmly into the top layer of the hard soil. The push-pull action dragged his scrawny body across the damp earth—one inch at a time. Caught in the motion his broken arm was pulled along beneath his weight and he groaned with pain. When he finally caught his breath again, he turned his eyes in the direction of the road where another car just flew by. Again his left leg curled up into position followed by his outstretched arm. With his eyes pinned on the prize he drew in a shallow breath and pushed his body forward again. The familiar agony flooded his body once more. Except, this time he didn't flinch. He had shut his mind off to receiving it and kept his eyes firmly on the road ahead. Just like he had done all those times he was the receiver of his father's wrath. It instantly surprised him that he suddenly had an over-whelming will to survive. To live. Why, he didn't quite know. But he wasn't about to give up without a fight.

The short distance to the road would have taken less than a minute had he been able to walk it. Instead he had only gained a few inches at a time. There was no way of telling how many hours it had taken him to haul his near-lifeless body across the uneven dirt. But what he did know was that the time between passing vehicles had increased. As the cars became fewer, it was clear that his hope of being rescued was slowly slipping away with each passing second. Until the cars eventually stopped altogether.

The night grew eerily quiet. His body no longer felt the icy winter air that pushed through the thin fabric of his tee shirt. Somehow his body had adapted to the near-freezing temperature. Or perhaps he was already dead.

He forced his heavy eyelids open. Inches away from his nose his left hand stared back at him. Dark red patches of dried blood mixed with dirt lay in a thick crust around each finger. On two of his fingers his nails had chafed away to expose his flesh; evidence of how hard he had already fought to stay alive. Lucky Lenny refused to believe his luck had run out. He'd wait. For however long it took to be found. All he needed to do was stay awake. Stay alive.

WHILE HIS BODY NOW LAY HALFWAY OVER THE RIDGE where the dirt met the tarmac, sprawled like the crime scene sketches on his favorite detective show, he started to question the purpose of life. His life, to be more exact. Had he squandered valuable opportunities that had already come his way? Was spinning the wheel of fortune all his life amounted to? Who decided that for him anyway? His alcoholic father who'd beat him to a pulp just for the fun of it. Or his weak mother who'd finally had the nerve to defend herself. It's not as if he had planned to be born into this empty world that had never once dealt him a decent hand. But there he was. Born to be someone's punching bag. A tool that qualified his pathetic father to claim his drinking money through state grants. No, Lucky Lenny was everything but lucky. Every opportunity that had ever come his way he had meticulously planned. He had always created his own plans. Big plans. The last of which was meant to be the final payoff that would've set him up for the rest of his life. A chance to get away from his cursed existence. Yet, with all the odds stacked in his favor, his plan had failed. Or had it? Lenny paused to mull over his thoughts. Even if he did somehow survive this horrible twist of his fate, could he go back to a life that relied solely on luck? Did he want to?

And as he once again pondered the meaning of his shabby life, with his ear flush against the near-frosted tarmac, the faintest of vibrations drove into his eardrum. At first, he thought he was imagining it. But then it grew louder and louder. Until the wheels of a car screeched to a standstill right beside his head. Suddenly fear reared its ugly head. What if they had come back to make sure he was dead? What if they, in the interim, had discovered he knew more than he had let on?

But as quickly as panic tried to take over his broken body, something else, something far more powerful than fear, overwhelmed his senses. For the first time, he experienced hope. Not the superficial hope he felt each time he rolled the dice. True hope. The kind of hope that told him he had a chance to do things differently. A chance to do things right. A chance that had nothing to do with luck, and everything to do with survival.

The male voice next to his ear was calm and reassuring. Nothing more than a faint whisper. What Lenny imagined an angel would sound like. Not that he believed in heavenly beings of any kind. But he believed it when this voice told him he would live and that everything was going to be just fine.

CHAPTER TWO

W hen Lenny came to he was lying in a hospital bed, alone in the room. His broken arm had been neatly set in a cast and his other hand's fingertips bandaged. When he tried to sit up he cringed with pain.

"Oh, you shouldn't be moving. I'll call the nurse."

A female voice from the far corner startled him. She had dashed out the door screaming, 'he's awake!' before he even had a chance to speak to her. Moments later a nurse hurriedly entered the room.

"Well, hello there. You are one lucky man. In all my years I have never quite seen anyone survive as many injuries as these. It seems the big man up there isn't quite finished with you. Any idea who did this to you?" The upbeat nurse ended with a question.

He shook his head and looked over to the wide-eyed

young woman who now stood in the corridor and peered through the small window in the door.

"That's Jo. She's one of our more regular in-treatment patients here. She's got a bit of a curious streak, that one; but she's totally harmless. Visiting the patients keeps her mind off the cancer. Of course, it doesn't help that no one knows how you got yourself to the front steps or that we've been forced to keep you sedated for an entire week. The mystery has been driving her mad. If she bothers you just let me know," the nurse said with a smile.

"What's your name?" she probed as she inserted a needle into the IV bag and rolled her thumb over the valve below it.

"Lenny."

"Well, Lenny, is there someone you'd like us to call? Any family members?"

He paused for a few moments. There was, but there was no way she'd come.

He shook his head.

"All right then. I've just given you something extra to control the pain. You should feel it kick in anytime now. Your vitals are fine but surviving seventeen stab wounds is going to take a little more time to recover from. Somehow they had missed all your vital organs. That in itself is a miracle. Dr. Munroe said you should make a full recovery now that most of the infection has settled down. You might have already noticed that you're able to move your right leg now too." She smiled then continued. "The paralysis was only temporary because of the swelling. But you're stuck here for a bit I'm afraid. Just to give the wounds enough time to heal." She turned to leave but then stopped and looked back at him.

"Oh, and the police will be here soon."

"The police? Why?"

"Don't you want to find out who did this to you? We had a duty to report it. It's just a routine visit. I doubt you'll ever get your wallet or whatever else they stole back, but it can't hurt to try. I'll be back to check on you in a little while. Get some rest."

The news left Lenny anxious. If the police got involved he'd end up back in the slammer. He couldn't risk that. Right now they'd suspect he was mugged. He had to keep it that way. But once the police questioned him they'd expect him to provide them with his full name and social security number. Then it would definitely be game over. He couldn't let that happen. He'd worked far too hard to become a snitch or end up spending the rest of his life behind bars. All he needed was one sweet deal and a ticket to Mexico.

The tempting thought was enough motivation to have him fling back the covers and swing his legs over the side of the bed. Using his teeth he yanked the IV tube from his arm. Whatever the nurse had injected was strong enough to have numbed most of his pain. It should buy him enough time to get away. Halfway between the bed and the door, he realized the hospital gown wasn't going to do it and he flung open the nearby locker door. It was empty. He hurried back over to the steel cabinet next to the bed and pulled open the single drawer. His eyes lingered on the blue Bible. It wasn't the Bible itself that had brought him to pause. The big, bold, red words written on a tract that lay next to it held his attention.

'Luck or Design? Is your life all it's meant to be?'

He thought about the question for a second then clumsily snatched it up between his bandaged fingers. Somewhere deep inside him, it struck a chord. Closing his fist over the tract he stuffed it inside the hollow of his cast where it folded over his palm, then headed toward the door. A stealthy look outside his room told him the coast was clear. He remembered the girl, Jo, and found himself wishing upon the universe that she'd be nosying around somewhere else right now. As he made his way up the corridor he caught sight of a door marked 'Medical Personnel Only.' Two chatty nurses emerged from behind the door and he quickly sat down on a nearby empty wheelchair. When they had left, he slipped inside.

"Jackpot!" he exclaimed under his breath.

It was the staff locker room. He hastily moved

between the lockers in search of clothing, relieved when he found a pair of men's jeans and a dark green sweater. Changing into the clothes with a broken arm proved to be much harder than he'd anticipated. Two lockers further down he slipped a pair of trainers on and was good to go.

Satisfied freedom was within reach, he helped himself to a faded yellow baseball cap that dangled from a hook on the wall on the way out.

At the end of the corridor, he turned the corner where he had just passed the nurses' station and almost bumped into two police officers who were heading toward the nurse on duty. He heard them announce they were there for the mystery guy who'd got mugged. Lenny increased his pace, deciding to take the stairwell down instead. Once through the door, he descended two steps at a time, wincing each time his feet hit the hard surface. Another flight of stairs delivered him to an area where two paramedics burst through a double door in front of him, pushing a gurney past him into a giant elevator to his left. Caught up in the trauma they barely took notice of him as he slipped through the double doors and made his escape between several parked ambulances.

THE TRUCK DRIVER DIDN'T ASK ANY QUESTIONS WHEN Lenny begged him for a lift into the city. He knew not to. People hitched rides with him all the time. Most of them were troubled teens. The less he knew the better. As agreed, the trucker dropped Lenny at the service station a few blocks away from home. By the time Lenny got to his front door, he was totally worn out and in dire need of more of whatever the nurse had injected earlier. But at least he was home.

Lenny lived alone in a derelict two-bedroom government house in a seedy part of town on the outskirts of Atlanta. The sitting room was, as always, a mess. Old pizza boxes, some with rotten, moldy left-overs, lay scattered throughout the tiny house. A few dozen empty beer bottles were strewn all over the stained mustard-colored carpet and stale cigarette smoke lay thick in the air. As was to be expected, the kitchen had a stench so foul that, even with the window open, it took your breath away. But none of it bothered Lenny much at all. He went straight for the rusty fridge and scooped up a six-pack of beers with his one arm. As he flopped down into the sagging brown sofa he somehow knew exactly where to find the tv remote under a stack of old newspapers on the floor.

"Lucky Lenny is back, baby!" he announced out loud to the sports commentator on the betting channel.

He gulped down four large swigs of beer and reached for the cordless phone stuck between the two cushions of the couch. His thumb quickly moved over the buttons before he wedged the phone between his cheek and his shoulder.

"Hey, it's me. Could you help out an old friend? Have I ever let you down, huh? Who was there for you when you first started out in this neighborhood, huh? That's right, me. I don't need much. Ten large on number three for tonight. Of course I'm sure. Call it a hunch. Don't worry, Dutchy. Lucky Lenny is feeling very lucky tonight. How long have we known each other, huh? I told you I'm good for it. I just need a little more time. Hey, who took the heat when your son got himself into trouble, huh? I lost my job because of that. Fine, fifteen percent, but not a penny more. Attaboy. I owe you, buddy."

Lenny hung up the phone and opened another beer. He stripped down to his underwear and settled back in on the sofa, his eyes glued to the horses as they lined up behind the gates. His eye caught the corner of the tract where it poked out from underneath his cast. As he recalled the words he sucked air through the tiny gap between his two front teeth. '*Luck or Design?*' What did that even mean? Luck he knew all too well. He wasn't dubbed Lucky Lenny without reason. But design? Designed by who? God? He highly doubted that. His very existence was nothing more than an accident. A product of a drunken loser who'd had his evil ways with his mother. Nothing about that was designed. He pushed the piece of paper back in place and focused his attention on the horses instead. That was something he could believe in.

The gates flew open and Lenny leaned forward in anticipation of a win. But as his luck would have it, his horse didn't even place. He swore under his breath and tossed his bottle of beer against the wall behind the television set. That was his last chance, his only hope of getting himself out of this mess he'd somehow managed to land himself in. Moments later his phone rang. He knew who it was so he didn't answer. Suddenly the walls started closing in on him. Just a few short moments ago he'd felt on top of the world. Now he'd sunk back into the bottomless pit he had spent most of his life in. He plucked at the bandage that wrapped around most of his torso. It felt tight and suffocating. He'd have to have another go at it. As soon as the day broke he'd head downtown. All he needed was to deliver one more package. Actually deliver it.

CHAPTER THREE

He pulled the collar of his black leather jacket over his mouth and tucked his left hand into the pocket. The icy morning air on his skin had turned his fingers bright pink. His broken arm throbbed with pain. He had removed the sling to better hide his injury. Showing weakness and being vulnerable would only stunt his chances.

When he was almost at the usual meeting point under the bridge near the station, he stopped. He briefly threw his head back and closed his eyes. It was now or never. His last chance. He'd beg if he had to.

He smoothed his greasy hair back and took a deep breath, held it for a few seconds, and then set off down the path toward the bridge.

"Well, well, well. If it isn't the snake with the itchy

fingers." A tall dark-haired man in smart jeans and a black wool coat greeted him under the bridge.

"Hey, Diaz," he said sheepishly.

"You have quite the nerve showing your face here, Lenny."

"I know, I'm sorry."

"Yeah well, sorry ain't cutting it. Get lost."

"Please, I need this."

"You stole, Lenny! From one of my top clients. Not to mention that you stabbed me in the back. You nearly cost me my reputation."

"It won't happen again. I was stupid."

"You've got that right. Now scram. I have loyal runners arriving any second now."

"Please, Diaz, I need one more job. A big one. I owe a lot of people money."

Diaz threw his head back as he bellowed a sadistic laugh then ejected a ball of saliva at Lenny's feet.

"You're scum, Lenny! They should've killed you. *I* should kill you!"

"Oh they tried, believe me. Where do you think I've been the last week? Fighting for my life in the hospital, that's where," he answered his own question in an effort to conceal his nerves.

Diaz didn't say anything. He just stared into Lenny's eyes.

"So you've finally run out of that luck you keep talking about. Desperate then, aren't you?"

Lenny nodded.

"Very."

"How do I know I can trust you?"

"Look at me, Diaz. I have nothing left to lose. I almost died, man. I have every bookie between here and Vegas out to get me. I need this job. This is my only hope of staying alive. I need the money."

Diaz drew the mucus in his nose to the back of his throat, his eyes never leaving Lenny's.

"How much are you in for?"

"Quarter of a million."

A smug look in Diaz's eyes preceded a wide grin that displayed a mixture of pleasure and surprise. Seconds later he pulled out his mobile phone and pulled one leather glove off with his teeth before gliding his thumb up and down the screen, glancing Lenny's way every few seconds.

"Let's see how lucky you really are, Lenny. If you can pull this one off you're in for a cool million payday. Mess it up and I'll be spitting on your grave."

"You won't regret it, Diaz, I promise! You can count on me. Thank you… thank you. I won't let you down."

"Yeah, whatever. Spare me the soppy gratitude. Get on with it. You'll find your burner at the pickup. Your keywords are strawberries and champagne. And, Lenny, if you get caught, you keep your trap shut, understand. Or I'll make sure you won't live another day this time."

Lenny nodded and quickly turned to walk away.

En route to the pickup, he had a newfound spring in his step. He had done it once again. Somehow he had managed to talk his way into another opportunity. He found himself smiling as if he had already collected the million-dollar payment. Mexico was one drop-off away from happening. He'd pay off everyone he owed and hop on the next plane out of there.

"Who's designing now, huh?" he shouted up toward the heavens.

THE PICKUP WAS A NEWSSTAND IN DOWNTOWN Atlanta. He waited until there were no customers and walked up to the girl who sat behind the glass window. Looking over his shoulder he used their code phrase.

"It's a great day for a picnic, isn't it?"

The girl with the bleach-blonde hair looked up from her gossip magazine and blew a bright pink bubblegum bubble between her dark purple lips. She popped the bubble with one matching purple fingernail before twirling the stretchy candy around her finger.

"Oh yeah? And what would you have in your picnic basket?"

"Strawberries and champagne."

The girl stopped playing with her gum midway between twirls and looked at him as if she'd just seen a ghost. She sat like that for at least five seconds, not saying a word.

"Strawberries and champagne," Lenny repeated, looking over his shoulder again.

"I'm not deaf, you know. I just can't believe what I'm hearing."

"What do you mean? Why?"

"You don't know. Boy, then you're an even bigger fool than you look."

"Know what?"

She snickered as she reached for a newspaper and quickly buried the disposable mobile phone between the layers before she slid it through the opening in the window.

"Know what? Tell me," Lenny pushed again.

"Have a great picnic. I would have said you should let me know how it goes, but it's pointless. You won't make it back here."

There was no time for Lenny to get her to explain what she meant before a fat, bald guy suddenly stood peering over his shoulder.

The girl's comment had Lenny somewhat on edge as he made his way back to his apartment to wait for further instructions. What didn't she tell him? Why did she think he was a fool?

A FEW SHORT BLOCKS FROM HIS HOUSE HE HAD forgotten about the stupid girl's comments. What did she know anyhow? She was just the contact who handed out the burner phones. His mind was firmly focused on Mexico. That's all he cared about right now. He'd wait at his apartment for the instruction to come through, deliver the package, and collect his money. Nothing a regular courier guy didn't already do. How hard could it be? This time next week he'd be on a Mexican beach soaking up the sun.

He popped into the drug store down the street from his house and bought some painkillers. When he exited the shop he spotted the black SUV with the gold gorilla sticker on the rear. It was Dutch's boys. They'd come to collect the ten grand he had lost the previous night. So he popped back into the shop to wait it out.

"If you're not buying you need to get out, please."

The man behind the counter shouted at him.

"I wasn't born yesterday, son. You're either planning to shoplift or you're hiding from someone. I don't want any trouble in my store. Get out before I call the police."

"Fine, cool it, old man. Can I slip out the back?" Lenny nervously peered out into the street and saw they had parked outside his house. His eyes begged the store owner to cut him some slack.

Relieved to have the man push his chin up in the direction of the back exit, Lenny dashed toward it and hid in the alley behind the dumpsters.

When he was certain Dutch's men had left and it was safe to go home, he slipped in through the bathroom window at the back of his house. Beer in hand on his sofa, he flipped the burner phone's cover open to reveal the screen, hoping to find a message. Dutch's goons would be back by morning. Of that, he was very certain. They and the other dozen goons that were after him. His body hurt terribly so he washed two painkillers down with his beer and rested his head back against the couch. The cast made the inside of his arm itch and he grunted in annoyance. He remembered when his father threw him against the wall when he was thirteen. It was the first time he had fractured his arm. It was summertime and his arm had itched like mad. His sister had stuck a knitting needle between the cast and his arm to help him get rid of the itch. It was a genius idea. He hadn't seen her since their mother died. She was always the smart one. Talk about planning. She had it all worked out. When she first started entering beauty pageants he had made fun of her. But then she started winning and it became harder and harder to hide it from their father. So, in exchange for helping her keep it a secret—and taking most of the punishment that came when their father did find out—she shared the prize money with him. They used to pretend he was her bodyguard. But unlike Lenny, she had stashed all her prize money away until she finally had enough, and ran away the moment she turned eighteen. They had remained in contact. She'd even helped him out a couple of times with a few small loans. Loans he never paid back. And when he finally got caught and was put in the slammer, he never heard from her again. Apart from the time their mother died and she personally delivered the news to him in prison. That was the last time he'd seen her. A couple of years later he happened to spot her photo in the newspaper. She had married some local councilman in an over-the-top soiree in Charleston. She looked happier than he had ever seen her look before. True happiness. The kind he would only know once he sat on that beach in Mexico.

Lenny's mind was still on his sister and the meaning of true happiness when the burner phone in his hand suddenly vibrated against his cast. But, as his eyes took in the message on the phone, an entirely different emotion overcame him. Instead of feeling excited over the opportunity that now knocked hard and fast on his door, the feeling in his gut said otherwise. Deep down in the pit of his stomach, something told him his route to happiness wasn't going to be an easy one. One that might very well end up in disaster or, at the very least, finally take his life.

CHAPTER FOUR

I f there was one thing Lenny wasn't, that was a coward. Except when it came to facing the loan sharks. That was a fight he knew he would never win. He slept with one eye open that night and made sure he was out the door before daybreak.

He had decided to wear his stolen hospital attire since the package had to be collected from an address on the more posh side of the city. It was important that he blended in as much as possible so he added a black dress jacket he had once bought when he managed to weasel his way into a private poker game. He even shaved. Yes, Lenny had it all planned out.

The message on the cell phone had told him to wait outside a tall, glass office building in the main business district. So he did, for almost forty minutes after the stipulated time. He checked one final time to see if he was at the correct address. He was. Just as he decided to head back home, another message buzzed on the phone. As if they knew he was about to leave.

The message told him to look for the park bench marked with a small white X in the nearby park where the package would be waiting for him.

It didn't take him long to locate the mark and he soon found a manila envelope stuck to the bottom of the seat. He quickly snuck it inside his jacket and waited for further instructions, but almost two hours later he still hadn't received a new message.

At the end of the path, he spotted a hot dog cart and finally gave in to his growling stomach. When he'd stuffed the last half of his second hot dog in his mouth, he stepped into the shadows of a secluded spot at the edge of a nearby office block and continued to wait. But another fifteen minutes later he had still not received any new instructions. It dawned on him that the address might have been marked on the envelope so he pulled it from his jacket and skimmed over the crumpled folds. Until then it hadn't even occurred to him that it might be written on the envelope. When he spotted the faint pencilled address written on the back his heart gave a jolt he was certain might have been a mini-stroke. His cheap gold watch showed it was just over two and a half hours since he had found the envelope. He swore under his breath. His oversight might have very well cost him the million dollars—and his life!

Irritated with himself he dashed across the street. The address was on the other side of town. There was no way he could walk it so he headed for the subway. Relieved to have been on time for the next departure he jumped on board the train and took a seat directly next to the exit doors. The train wasn't at all full, yet a very muscular Black man resembling a pro football player squashed into the two seats next to him. Lenny flinched as the man's big body shoved against his broken arm.

"Hey, watch it!" he said annoyed before popping two more painkillers in his mouth and forcing them down his dry throat without water. As he shut his eyes and put his head back waiting for them to take effect, the sharp prick of an insect on the side of his neck had him swing his left hand across to whack at it. Feeling uncomfortable and squashed next to the man he decided to move to the open seats opposite them but instantly felt dizzy as he did so. Moments later, Lenny fell to the floor.

"EXCUSE ME, SIR. THIS IS THE LAST STOP FOR THIS line," the male voice came as he repeatedly poked at Lenny's shoulder. "You can connect at 11th Street southbound."

Lenny didn't respond.

"Sir, wake up. You'll need to get off. It's the end of

the line," the conductor said again, this time, waking Lenny.

"Where am I? What happened?" Lenny said, confused and extremely groggy.

"If I had a dollar each time I get asked that," the conductor laughed. "The best nights out are the ones you can't remember. Perhaps you'll recall once you sleep it off. But, as curious as I am, you can't be doing that here. Come on."

The man helped Lenny to his feet and swung his arm around his waist to help him off the train.

"No wait, I'm not drunk," Lenny said as he resisted. "The package, where's the package?" He turned back to look on the seat when he didn't find it inside his jacket where he'd put it.

"Sir, please, you need to get off now."

"Someone took it. I was drugged. Someone drugged me and took the envelope," Lenny announced in a befuddled panic.

"I'm sure you left it in the last bar you were at. Now please go."

Now fully aware of the situation, Lenny ignored the conductor's pleas and dropped to his knees to search under the seats. But the package was gone.

Panic rushed through his body and sank to the bottom of his stomach as he reluctantly stepped off the train. The platform was quiet. His watch told him it was three a.m. When he'd got on the train earlier that day it wasn't even noon. He paced up and down the empty station, rubbing at the throbbing at his temples. Why would someone intentionally drug him to steal the package from him? How did they even know where he was? Was he followed? Nothing made any sense. Absentmindedly his hand reached for the itchy spot on his neck where he thought an insect had bitten him.

"Oh you stupid fool!" he shouted at himself as his fingers rubbed over the dried blood, realizing that it must have been the athletic man who had sat down next to him who had drugged him.

Now in a full-blown panic, he reached for the burner phone. There were five missed calls and more than a dozen messages. Beads of cold sweat perched above his worried eyebrows. He was a walking dead man. How could he have been so careless?

"Okay think, Lenny, think," he said out loud as he anxiously paced back and forth. "Just tell them the truth, that's all. This was not your fault. Nothing you can't talk yourself out of," he said out loud again then turned to head to the stairwell. As he prepared to head up the stairs a raspy voice came from the dark shadows beneath the stairwell and scared him witless.

"You can run but he'll keep coming for you, you know."

The words stopped Lenny dead in his tracks.

"Who's there?"

"You can feel it, can't you?"

"If you have something to say come out and face me like a man! I'm not afraid of you," Lenny shouted, still paused at the bottom of the stairs.

The voice went quiet and Lenny stepped back onto the platform. Convinced it was one of Diaz's men, he struggled to control his breathing. Every cell in his scrawny body was on high alert, his body tense with fear. When the voice remained silent, he decided to move toward it, briefly looking behind him to make sure he wasn't being ambushed. But the station was completely deserted.

Bent at the waist he anxiously searched the dark corners beneath the stairwell, his heart pounding hard in his chest. In the shadows, he spotted the figure of a man lying on the floor against the wall. For fear of it being a trap, he paused a long second before he bravely took another two steps toward the shadowy nook beneath the stairs. As his eyes adjusted to the darkness he saw that it was just a homeless person sheltering there for the night. Annoyed at the distraction he made a clicking sound with his tongue against his teeth and turned back toward the stairwell.

"It's all planned, you know," the homeless man's gentle voice echoed behind him.

Again it brought Lenny to a halt.

"What do you want, huh? Money? Stand in line, pal! I don't have any okay?" Lenny shouted out in frustration.

"He can help you if you let him."

"Oh come on, old man. Stop talking crazy. I have better things to do than to listen to this."

Lenny was irritated, and he spat a few more unsavory words at the man. But as hard as he tried to turn away and run up those stairs, he couldn't. It was as if an unknown, invisible force had paralyzed his legs. Wanting him to hear more. Angry frustration bubbled up inside his body as his soul wrestled with his mind. Exhausted and confused he leaned his head toward the staircase's railing and rested his head on his broken arm.

"Bones will grow back by themselves, but it's what you've got hurting inside that needs true healing," the drifter said referring to his broken arm.

"Is that so?"

"It is. It's time to face the truth."

"Yeah well, the truth is exactly what's going to get me killed."

"Sometimes we have to go through the desert before we get to the Promised Land."

The man's statement forced Lenny's emotions into overdrive and he flung his body back to come face-to-face with the vagrant under the staircase.

"Now I know you're insane. You're talking as if you know what I'm going through. Well, you don't! My entire life has been a desert. One big, barren, godless desert! This was my chance to get to this *Promised Land* fools like you always talk about. Mexico was my

Promised Land. And now I'll never see it. It doesn't matter how hard I try to get there, I never do! I'm tired of this life and I'm tired of listening to your psychobabble as if you know what you're talking about. You don't, okay! We live off scraps, like the scavengers at the bottom of the ocean, just to survive. Just so the big sharks of this world don't have to go through the deserts. Newsflash, old man. There is no Promised Land. And there never will be for people like you and me!"

With his cursing words still echoing through the empty station, torment lying shallow in his eyes, Lenny turned and escaped up the stairs. Never once looking back, never once stopping.

CHAPTER FIVE

Lenny's feet hit the quiet sidewalk with force. A force driven by decades of anger and pain. He ran as fast as his weak body would let him. But try as he might, he couldn't get the vagrant's words out of his mind. Like a lingering sore pestering his soul, it ate away at him. Stride by stride. And even when his lungs burned from the icy winter air, and his legs threatened to give way beneath his exhausted body, he couldn't stop running. He didn't quite know what or who he was running away from, or where he was running to, but he kept going. Perhaps it was his own demons chasing him. Or perhaps he thought he could run his way into the Promised Land. All he knew was that he didn't care anymore. Something deep inside him had given up.

When his body finally collapsed and he fell to the cold, hard ground like a puppet whose strings had snapped, he sobbed uncontrollably. He sobbed about his childhood, about his miserable life, and the desert he could never seem to escape. Until he had no more tears left to cry. And when he finally found the will to pick his near-frozen body up off the sidewalk, the first golden rays of the morning poured onto his face. And though he couldn't be certain, he thought he heard the same male voice that had rescued him from the side of the road, tenderly whisper in his ear, *Everything will be all right.*

Desperate to believe in life, in hope, in something, Lenny clung to the gentle words that were spoken as he made his way back to his home. And even though he knew trouble would surely be waiting for him, he also knew he had nowhere else to go. If Dutch's men, or perhaps even Diaz himself were there waiting for him, he'd let them have their way. But he couldn't run anymore. He had nowhere left to hide. He'd take whatever cards life now dealt him—even if it was death.

Just a few blocks away from home, when his mind was still occupied with what to do once he got there, he briefly let his guard down. Taken by surprise, a black minivan screeched to a halt next to him. In the flurry of movement two burly men whose faces he didn't see, pulled a black hood over his head, and threw him into the van. They didn't speak at all. Just shoved him hard against the steel floor. When he tried to straighten up a strong hand shoved a wet cloth over his mouth, pressing it down over his jaw.

And Lenny was once again forced into a transient world of darkness as the chloroform took effect.

THERE WAS A BRIEF MOMENT WHEN DISAPPOINTMENT flooded his insides as Lenny opened his eyes to find himself alive. But there he was again, the one who keeps surviving. His eyes scanned the space around him. It was poorly lit with a few rays of sunlight spilling in through the cracks of three brown-tinted windows. Positioned at the top of the wall where it met the thick steel rafters of a pointy roof, the window let just enough light in for him to take in the room. He was tethered at the waist to a single wooden chair that stood in the middle of what appeared to have once been some kind of old clothing factory; an assumption he made when he spotted several damaged dress forms piled on top of each other in a corner. Next to them was a large table upon which about half a dozen industrial sewing machines sat crammed together. The filthy tiled floor had broken and missed tiles in several places, and the whole space smelled moldy. He listened for voices or movement of any kind, but there were none. He was alone. He peered up at the broken windows and saw that the sky was hues of bright amber. Concluding it was probably nightfall, he tried wriggling his body to loosen the several strands of chains that were twisted around his torso and legs, then around the backrest and legs of the chair. They didn't budge.

He was stuck, confined to a chair, helplessly waiting. With his hands tied together in his lap, he tried to twist his arm to see what time it was. They had taken his watch—or perhaps it got lost during his capture. His eye caught the slightest bit of one of the red letters on the tract that somehow had managed to stay in its hiding place inside his cast. Every morsel of his being wanted to rip it to shreds. Just thinking about it made him angry all over again. Ever since he had found it, all it had done was mess with his mind, caused his luck to change.

Eager to force his mind away from the piece of writing, he leaned back to look over his shoulder. In the far corner, he could see a door; plain, and made from ordinary plywood with no lock. He thought of shuffling the chair to the door and attempting to open it with his mouth, but decided against it. It would be pointless since he'd still be in chains and had no way of knowing what awaited him on the other side of the door.

So he decided to wait it out.

HE HAD NO IDEA HOW LONG HE HAD BEEN SITTING there. The amber sky had turned to midnight blue and the temperature inside the building had dropped to what he felt was near freezing. If nothing else, that alone was torture. Freezing to death, and the relentless waiting for the unknown. But eventually, he managed to fall asleep only to be woken by the slow pouring out of a bucket of icy water over his face. The cold sent shockwaves through his entire body and left behind a dull pain in his forehead. It took several attempts for him to catch his breath and rid his aching eyes from the water. Soon after the bucket had run empty, and he could finally see again, he lifted his head. Standing in his long black wool coat and shiny black shoes, he recognized Diaz's tall silhouette towering over him.

"You just couldn't help yourself now, could you, Lenny?"

"I didn't do it."

"Oh, but you did, Lenny. And here we are, right back where we started."

"Diaz, I swear, I didn't take it. I was drugged and—"

"Save it, Lenny. You're a greedy, little snake, and I told you I'd kill you myself if you ever took from me again. Didn't I?"

Lenny didn't react. He wasn't sure if there was anything he could say to convince Diaz he'd had nothing to do with the lost package.

"So tell me, Lenny. How much did they offer you, huh?"

"What? No, I wasn't offered anything. Someone stole it from me."

"Oh, come on, Lenny. Just how stupid do you think I

am, huh? Fool me once, fool me twice, right? How much?"

Lenny's heart dropped to the pit of his stomach.

"I didn't get any money, Diaz. I swear. I didn't take the package. I was on the train and a big Black guy jabbed a needle in my neck. Next thing I know I'm being woken up by the conductor at three a.m. and the envelope is gone. That's the truth. I swear on my mother's grave."

Diaz turned his back on Lenny and made several sucking noises through his teeth.

"You see, Lenny. I'd have believed you if this was the first time you'd double-crossed me. But you can understand why I find it really hard to believe some strange guy on a train drugged you and stole my package."

Diaz peered into his eyes.

"Why? Why would you steal from me again? I mean, it's not as if the paycheck wasn't more than substantial. Heck, it's the biggest one on my list. And for good reason. That package carried something of significant value. So how much did it take for you to stab me in the back again, Lenny? Just how much did you value your life at, huh?"

Lenny dropped his head to his chest and then sideways onto his shoulder.

"I can prove it. Look on the side of my neck. You'll

find the injection mark. Look!" he shouted when Diaz didn't immediately react.

Diaz pushed out his chin toward one of his henchmen who stood behind Lenny. A quick second later the man had a flashlight aimed at Lenny's neck. A silent nod in Diaz's direction had him confirm that there was indeed a needle mark. The man assumed his position two steps behind him.

"See, I told you. I'm telling you the truth. I didn't take your package."

Diaz stared silently into his eyes. As if trying to look into Lenny's soul.

"How do I know you didn't shoot up?"

"Drugs! Really? I don't do drugs. I've never touched the stuff. Someone knocked me out, Diaz. Someone who knew I had the package. Please, you have to believe me. I needed this job, Diaz. I needed this money. If anything, they stole from *me*."

Diaz let out a loud laugh.

"That's so typical of you, is't it, Lenny? Always an answer for everything."

He moved closer and squatted so that his eyes lined up with Lenny's.

"Tell you what, *Lucky* Lenny. Let's see how bad you really want the money, shall we?"

He pushed his chin out again towards his sidekick who handed him a newspaper. When Diaz stood up he turned his back on Lenny and opened the newspaper as if he was going to read from it.

"You see, Lenny. When you came back begging for another job, I decided to make sure I took out a little insurance policy. Just in case you crossed me again. So I did a bit of digging around. It seems you have a lot to lose. Actually, you made it really easy for me."

Diaz turned to face Lenny, his eyes dripping with self-satisfaction. He held up the newspaper to where he had folded it open to a big black and white photo that took up the entire top half of the page.

It was as if someone had taken their ice cold hands and wrapped them around Lenny's neck, slowly squeezing the life out of him. As his eyes skimmed over the photo and the small caption beneath the image, shock turned to fury. But though Lenny had had a lifetime of practice to maintain a poker face, this one time that he needed it most, he couldn't.

"Leave my sister out of this," he said in the lowest of whispers through a clenched jaw.

Diaz folded the paper and tossed it in Lenny's lap. As if to further emphasize his intentions.

"Diaz, I swear. You touch my sister and I'll kill you with my bare hands. You hear me?"

But Diaz had already turned to leave the room.

"Diaz! Leave her alone! I'll get the stinking package back, but you leave my sister alone!" he shouted after him.

"You have seventy-two-hours, Lenny, or you both die," Diaz said calmly over his shoulder as he walked away.

And when Diaz shut the door behind him, a single blow of his crony's fist knocked Lenny's lights out.

CHAPTER SIX

F aint rays of sunlight poured through the broken windows high above his head as Lenny once again woke to a new sunrise. He was no longer sitting in the wooden chair. He was no longer chained up. Instead, he was lying on the filthy tiled floor next to it. As he slowly sat up, one hand instinctively reaching for his throbbing jaw, he picked up the newspaper that had been neatly placed next to him; a reminder of what was at stake. As if Lenny wasn't acutely aware. He unfolded the paper to read the full article. The photo had been taken at a governors' charity ball in Wilmington, North Carolina a week earlier. Carrie looked like a princess, glowing in a beaded crystal ball gown, beside her husband. Like a real-life Cinderella. Happier than he had ever seen her before. A tiny smile emerged at the corner of his mouth as he recalled her playing with the princess doll she had gotten for her fifth birthday. She had always dreamed of being swept off her feet by a prince and dancing the night away at their wedding ball. This sure came close to that. The memory left him smiling, but he quickly drew his attention back to the article. It told him that her husband was the mayor of the nearby small coastal town that went by the name of Turtle Cove. The next sentence left him ice cold.

The mayoral couple will be hosting the town's annual Christmas Tree *Switching on the Lights Festival*.

He stared at the date next to it. It was tomorrow. There was no time to waste. He'd have to get down there before Diaz got to her first. There was no telling what he'd do to her to punish him.

He ripped the article away from the rest of the paper, scrunching it up as he stuffed it inside the pocket of his pants while he stumbled to his feet. Somewhat dizzy from the lack of food and water, he made for the door. When he finally found his way outside through a maze of corridors and two flights of stairs, he found himself outside a deserted plant in the middle of nowhere. He picked a direction and began jogging down the overgrown road. The sand was thick and loose as if he were running along a beach. It took every bit of strength to keep his feet steady and his face from planting into the ground. There was a moment where he pretended he was running on the beach in Mexico, the sunrise full in his face. Just so he could keep his mind off the agony his body was enduring. He was dehydrated and beyond the point of exhaustion, but he kept running, stopping to catch his breath every minute or so. He had to get to Carrie before they did.

Dread rushed through his veins as the thought of his sister ending up dead in a ditch somewhere settled in his mind. He would never forgive himself if something happened to her because of him. She didn't deserve it.

In the far distance, he heard traffic so he briefly stopped to listen more closely. Determining he was running towards it he pushed on. Before long, the sandy road changed to gravel, and soon after that, his feet hit the tarmac.

He quickly tucked in his shirt and smoothed down his greasy hair. With one thumb out he tried to look respectable and confident in the hope that a car would stop and pick him up. He recognized the road to be one that was leading out of the city towards Charlotte. It was way off course. But if he could hitch a ride back toward the interstate he could catch a ride southbound from there.

The coast was at least six hours away by car. Catching a lift with a trucker would take twice as long when adding in all their mandatory stops along the way. There was only one way he'd get to warn Carrie before they got to her first and that was by traveling in his own vehicle. One he, of course, didn't own. Deciding not to waste any more time, he continued walking backward while holding out his thumb, his eyes pleading. Several vehicles had passed him by without heeding his need for help, but he kept going. It must have been another twenty minutes of slow walking when at long last a banged-up wood-paneled pickup truck pulled up in front of him.

The blonde-haired man, roughly in his fifties, rolled his window down—only about ten inches. He was friendly but cautious. On the seat next to him was a well-worn straw hat, a half-eaten sandwich, and a flask. A quick conversation through the small opening of his window and Lenny was invited to jump on the back of his truck.

Huddled between a couple of collapsing hay bales, Lenny welcomed the chance to rest. He realized he must have dozed off as he jerked awake when the driver rapped loudly against the window pane between them. He had pulled over at the edge of a small drive-through town just as they had agreed. And while most in Lenny's position would have preferred to be dropped closer to the city, Lenny knew exactly what he was doing, and where he was going.

As he rounded the service station he spotted the orange and blue bunting of the car dealership. He had once or twice played a game of underground poker with its owner. Cactus Jack, a name he fondly went by, was a stocky, partially bald man who, for the most part, lived a respectable life—at least as far as his community was aware. But once a month he'd sneak off to an illegal game of cards in the city and let what was left of the patches of hair above his small ears down. His love for cars was as brazen as his love for the tacky gold jewelry that adorned his pudgy neck and fingers. But Cactus Jack had another weakness. He also loved his women. Problem was, he had been 'happily' married to Irene for most of his life. And Irene's well-to-do daddy owned forty percent of his business. So when Lenny had accidentally caught him living on the edge with a pretty girl half his age after a round of poker one night, Jack had made him promise not to tell his wife—or anyone else. A pact Lenny was all too happy to make at the time and a favor he had saved calling in for precisely an occasion like this.

When Cactus Jack spotted Lenny's disheveled presence roaming outside his office between the vehicles, he instantly knew the day had come. Like a bullet from a gun, he jumped up from behind his desk and dashed across the small showroom to meet Lenny out front before any of his salesmen could get to him.

"Hey, if it isn't my old friend Lucky Lenny," he said with fake sincerity. "Long time no see."

"It's been a while, yes. How's that wife of yours?" Lenny went in for the kill. Time was of the essence.

"Well, she's great, thank you for asking, Lenny." Cactus Jack tried to conceal his discomfort with his equally feigned reply, but he knew full well where Lenny was heading. The beads of sweat on his toad-like face revealed all. He leaned in closer to make sure their conversation wouldn't be heard by one of his nearby salesmen.

"What do you want, Lenny? I know you're not here to buy a car."

Lenny smiled.

"I've come to call in that little debt you owe me. The one involving that young little thing you—"

"Okay, quiet. You don't have to announce it to the entire world you know. What do you want?"

"A car, with a full tank. And some fresh clothes and a bit of cash for the road."

Cactus Jack stood back and nervously sucked down on his top lip. A long second later he jiggled his waist-band over his fat tummy before settling his hands on his hips.

"Fine, but then my little indiscretion disappears for good. Forever, deal?"

"Deal."

"Stay here."

He waddled off with surprising agility for his partic-ular physique and returned a few moments later with a set of keys and five hundred dollars in cash.

"Take that one." He discreetly pushed his chin out

towards a shiny black Chevrolet Malibu. "She's not been added to the log yet. The tank is about a quarter full but the money should be more than enough to top it up. There's a shop down the road where you'll find your clothes and food."

Lenny flipped his fingers through the notes, looking up at Cactus Jack midway through.

"The guilt's been riding you I see."

"Yeah, yeah, whatever. Just take it and leave before someone catches us. I'll take care of the paperwork." He nudged Lenny lightly by the elbow.

"Pleasure doing business with you, Cactus Jack. I'll be seeing you, buddy."

And as a relieved Cactus Jack swiftly waddled back inside the safety of his office, Lenny pointed the nose of his new car toward the coast in search of his sister.

CHAPTER SEVEN

As was the case each year when this particular event came round, Turtle Cove was buzzing with excitement. Hundreds of holiday makers from all over the country had already taken up lodging in their vacation homes or one of the local tourist accommodations for their annual Christmas vacation.

It had been weeks of preparation building up to this night.

Against a backdrop of spectacular seasonal window displays in all the stores, strands of colorful lights were strung between the trees along the bustling sidewalks. Beginning at dusk, the small coastal town would fill with thousands of luminaries and the glow of the twinkling Christmas lights that adorned every business in town.

The center of town had been transformed into a

landscaped garden exhibit with lighted statues and animated Christmas displays programmed to illuminate to the sounds of holiday music. Free craft and interactive games tables lined the main road on both sides to form a colorful alley of festivities that would entertain the townspeople and the seasonal visitors every night leading up to Christmas Day; something that had become synonymous with Turtle Cove during the Christmas holidays.

In true form, with her clipboard in hand, by which she made sure everything went down without a hitch, Carrie Claiborne joyfully bounced between the community members, making notes along the way.

It was a clear but cold December evening and she was dressed in a pair of figure-hugging black slacks and a bright red, tailored coat tied at her waist, true to the spirit of the season. Her signature gloves matched her black pants and her iconic red lips were permanently pulled into a broad smile. Christmas was the happiest time of the year for her and she relished every minute of her duties as the town mayor's wife. She loved her life. And she loved her little girl.

"Careful, sweetheart, you're going to get a tummy ache if you eat another one. Not to mention that Mrs. Martins will have to whip up another batch of her delicious gingerbread men." She winked in approval at the baking shop owner when she wanted to sneak her daughter one last reindeer-shaped cookie.

"All right then, let's say thank you to Mrs. Martins and go see if Pastor Adam is done decorating the Christmas tree. We can't switch the lights on if there aren't any, can we?"

Carrie looked down at her daughter where she now skipped alongside her toward where the tree stood in the center of the small public garden. At almost nine years old, seeing her little girl so full of life and joy was the best feeling in the entire world. Maribelle meant everything to her and Carrie had worked hard to be the great mother she knew she was. The mother she had always longed for as a child. Each time she and Maribelle played together or hosted a tea party for her dozens of dolls, she remembered what her mother had never been. Her mother was weak. Not by design but by consequence. Too timid to stand up for herself and her two children. There were times she still felt guilty for all those occasions when she knew her mother had taken the blame for something she had done, but there were also those times she felt angry with her. Angry because she allowed it to happen. Angry because it took so long for her to fight back. Her mind traveled back to that night when she had been woken up by her parents' fighting. She had just turned eighteen and was only a few months away from graduating high school. Her brother had finally left home a few months before. She had quietly sneaked down the stairs to find her parents in a heated argument in the kitchen. Her father was shouting at her mother. He was drunk and had just come home after a night in the local bar. She remembered the punch that broke her mother's nose before he pinned her up against the wall by the neck. Carrie briefly shut her eyes as she recalled the wheezing noise that had come from her mother's throat as he was squeezing the breath out of her. And as she watched in horror while her mother's life slowly slipped away beneath her father's large hands, she had finally found her courage and run into the kitchen screaming for him to let her mother go. He didn't. Instead, her interference enraged him even further. That was the first and only time her father had hurt her. A forceful backhand that had sent her flying across the kitchen floor like a rag doll.

Something must have finally snapped in her mother when that happened. Something powerful enough to have made her reach for her kitchen scissors and kill her husband. One forceful strike into the side of his neck. The police ruled it self-defense and they didn't press charges. But her mother was never the same after that night. Life was never the same after that.

Carrie had tried many times to put her past behind her, forget it ever happened. But it kept coming up in her prayer time—especially of late. God's tender prompting through his spirit told her she still hadn't forgiven her father. Or her mother. She had locked it all up and thrown away the key. Far away where no-one could ever find it. Pretending none of her childhood ever existed was the only way she could forget.

And now, years later, Carrie had been given the chance to raise her own family. The right way. It was a far cry from the oppressed way she had grown up. It was the life she had always dreamed of living. The life she had been planning since she was just a little girl. But it didn't come easy and it didn't come without its sacrifices. Sacrifices that oftentimes were too much for her to bear. She thought of her big brother without whom she would've never been able to leave home. He had viciously suffered at the hands of their despicable excuse of a father for years so she and their mother wouldn't get hit. Guilt suddenly washed over her. She had even shut out her brother. The one person who didn't deserve it. She knew that. He was the only one who had always been there for her growing up, and she'd turned her back on him. She hadn't seen Leonard since the day she had visited him in prison to inform him of their mother's suicide. That was a long time ago.

"It's an angel, Mommy, a beautiful angel!" Maribelle's elated announcement at the Christmas tree topper jerked her back to the present. She pulled her mother by the hand toward where the town's natural Christmas tree stood tall in the center of the green space.

"Heavens to Betsy, would you look at that? It's an angel at the top of the tree."

Carrie knelt down next to Maribelle and shared in the moment that had her daughter in awe.

"It's perfect, Adam," Carrie said when he came out from behind the tree to stand next to them.

"So I did my job well then?" he asked Maribelle, kneeling beside her.

Since she and Abigail had been friends she was the closest he'd ever get to having a daughter again—a void he found particularly hard to fill during Christmas time. It had been almost two years since that tragic day.

"Yes, *very* well, Pastor Adam. I just wish Abi was here to see it too."

"I know. We all miss her but I think, if you look at that angel carefully, you'll notice it looks just like her. I'm certain she's sitting on Jesus' lap smiling down at you right now."

His words were exactly what Maribelle yearned to hear and she threw her arms around Adam's neck.

"Thank you, Adam. The tree looks spectacular," Carrie said before adding, "So are we all set for the switching-on ceremony at midnight?"

"Yup, I've checked every single globe myself. I need to nip back to the mission to make sure I'm set up for the service in the morning, but I'll meet you back here just before the ceremony. How about this little angel comes back with me to the Lighthouse so you can go about your business without interruptions? Elsbeth has the carolers running through a final choir practice and they were hoping to still find someone special enough who would volunteer to dress up as an angel and join them caroling a little later. I don't suppose you know of anyone who might fit the criteria?" Adam threw Carrie a sideways smile as he pretended to be serious.

"Oh, I can be an angel. Can I, Mommy, can I? I'll make the perfect angel. I can be special enough."

Carrie giggled.

"You already are, my sweetheart. You will make the most beautiful angel of all."

"Yippee! I'm an angel, I'm an angel!" Maribelle twirled around the tree.

"Then it's settled. Come on, little Christmas angel. We have to get your wings on," Adam said.

"Off you go then, my little Maribelle. I'll see you at the ceremony."

As Carrie watched her daughter bounce away with Adam, she turned to have one last look at the tree. From the corner of her eye, she noticed a tall dark figure leaning against the nearby swings. His arms were folded across his chest. He just stood there, watching her, staring at her. Her heart skipped several beats. She looked away and made a note to check in on the lanterns. As she adjusted one of the decorations on the tree Maribelle had played with, she looked up again. He was still there. His eerie presence made her uncomfortable. When she was done she turned to walk back up the green space—to pop in at Al's Hardware to check on the lanterns. Curiosity must have gotten the better of her because she caught herself glancing back over her shoulder again to see if the man was still there. He was.

She increased her pace. Why, she wasn't quite sure. But something felt off; left her unsettled. And as she moved up the slight incline toward the street she looked back at him once more. He was following her.

CHAPTER EIGHT

L enny flattened his foot on the Malibu's accelerator as soon as he hit the highway. He had stopped at a Chinese trading store where he bought a pair of khaki slacks, a navy sweater, and a navy puffer jacket. Afterward, he went to fill up the tank with gas and used the restroom to freshen up and change into his new clothes. He felt better than he had in days. Just before he turned onto the interstate, he popped through a fast-food drive-thru and ordered a large-sized portion of almost everything on the menu.

As he stuffed a handful of fries into his mouth he glanced at the clock on the dashboard. By his calculations, he should hit Wilmington before sunset. It was a straight six hours' drive and he didn't need to make anymore stops. From there he'd ask for directions to Turtle Cove. He'd make sure Carrie was safe and out of danger and then he'd retrace his steps to hunt down the package, starting with the girl at the newsstand. She clearly knew more than she'd been prepared to divulge. Diaz had given him three days to find the package. It was completely doable. Provided he got her to talk.

With a clear plan in mind, he turned on the radio and took a few large gulps of his soda before popping it back into the cupholder. A Johnny Cash song came on and he turned it up. He liked country music. Feeling upbeat, his thumbs tapped to the slow beat of the song. The song was about a lucky sun that had nothing to do but roll around in heaven. It spoke of the tears in his eyes, asked if the good Lord could hear him so he could wash his troubles away. The words suddenly struck a chord deep inside Lenny's soul. What if there really was a God who could hear him and wash all his troubles away? Could he be powerful enough to make everything disappear? Diaz, the bookies... everything that had haunted him all his life. He had never prayed before. Didn't even know how to. In fact, he had never really believed that there was a higher power. How could there be with all he'd had to endure in his life? The sudden shift in thought had him unexpectedly irritated and he slammed the radio button off. He turned his focus back to the road.

The highway was relatively free flowing so he shifted his body into a more relaxed seat. Easing into the drive, he settled at the maximum speed limit. He was cautious not to break it—the last thing he needed was to be pulled over for speeding. But in the pit of his stomach, he had a feeling of dread he just couldn't shake. His hands tightened over the wheel and he shuffled back into an upright position. Desperate to rid the tension he now felt in his chest, he rolled his shoulders back and cracked his neck sideways in both directions. Diaz had at least a three hour head start. He swore under his breath, annoyed at himself for wasting so much time on picking out clothing. But he knew why he had done that too. He wanted to look semi-decent when he saw her again. She had last seen him in an orange prison suit—not his best moment. He glanced at her photo in the newspaper. He had smoothed out the article on top of the dashboard in front of him. But the ball of tension remained in the pit of his stomach. He decided he needed to try and get there quicker. He knew Diaz wasn't a man who bluffed. So he pushed his foot down onto the accelerator, just enough to send him over the speed limit. Fifteen minutes later he heard the faint sound of police sirens somewhere in the distance behind him. His heart skipped a beat and he slammed his good hand down on the steering wheel, instantly regretting his decision to push the limit. He glanced back at the police vehicle that was closing the distance behind him. *Can't be caught! Not now!* His mind shifted into planning mode and he lifted his foot off the pedal instantly to reduce speed. He pulled into the middle lane and settled between two slower cars, both of which were also black. With any luck, the police wouldn't be able to tell which one had been speeding and pass him by. He tried to look casual as the police car came into view in his right rearview mirror. He stared straight ahead. From the corner of his eye, the blue lights flashed to his right but then flew past him.

"Yes!" he screamed victoriously out loud.

Less than a minute later another police vehicle zipped by followed by the paramedics. Soon after, the emergency response team followed suit. Something must have happened up front. Up ahead he could see the traffic starting to slow down.

"No, no, no! Keep moving," he said out loud as if they could hear him.

But before long he, along with all the other cars, had been brought to a dead standstill. And because he was in the middle lane, he was now wedged between both lanes of cars with no way out. He rolled his window down and popped his head out to see what had caused the sudden congestion. But he was too far back to see anything. He rolled his window up and took a few more bites of the half-eaten burger that he had left open on the passenger seat. Five minutes later the traffic had still not moved. By now he had turned his car off and his left knee was bouncing up and down from the pent-up stress.

"Come on, come on! What's the hold-up?"

He flipped the radio on and turned the dial to the traffic channel but there were no reports on his location. Deciding to leave it on nonetheless, he got out of the car and knocked on the window of the car next to him. Inside the senior couple seemed unperturbed by the delay. The woman was peacefully knitting away in the passenger seat while her husband sat quietly behind the wheel listening to the radio.

"Sorry to bother sir, ma'am, but I was wondering if you might know what's causing the delay?" Lenny asked through the half rolled down window.

Just as the old man was about to answer him the news report sounded over their radio. Together the trio listened as the broadcaster explained that an eighteen-wheeler had lost a tire and overturned, causing its entire load to spill across the highway.

"Great! Just what I needed," Lenny cried out in anger as he pushed himself away from the window.

"You know, dearie, sometimes these things happen for a reason," the old woman said in a wise tone.

Lenny had stepped back from the car into the narrow space between their vehicles and rubbed the back of his neck with his good hand.

"Yeah well, who decides that?"

"The Lord does, of course. He always has every-thing under control."

It wasn't what Lenny wanted to hear at that moment. He dropped his hand as if to swat away a fly and got back into his car, slamming his door loudly behind him. It was rude, he realized that, but he was beyond the point of irritation. He was livid. If he hadn't lingered in the Chinese store, hadn't taken so long to freshen up at the gas station, he would have missed it all. He would have been in time to get Carrie to safety. Now it might be too late.

Every cell in his body wanted to explode, be angry at someone. He slammed his hands down hard on the steering wheel, momentarily forgetting that his arm was broken. He winced with pain as his cast hit the wheel and sent vibrations through his broken bones.

"Aargh! Why is everything going wrong? Why can't it just go right for me, for once in my life, huh?" he shouted out at the universe. As if he expected an answer.

But when no answers came, he flopped his head forward onto the steering wheel; he had no choice but to wait it out. Lenny sat there in his car in total silence for the next two hours before the traffic finally started to move again. With his body upright leaning forward onto the steering wheel he pushed the car forward as fast as the congested traffic would allow. It took every ounce of willpower not to ram the car's nose into the back of the cars in front of him and push them out of the way.

"Move idiots!" he yelled in frustration when he saw the line in front of him snaked at least another half a mile.

When at long last his Chevrolet Malibu slowly glided past the accident scene on the highway, Lenny looked back at where the paramedics were lifting a covered body into the back of the ambulance. Pulled off onto the shoulder of the highway were two cars—both totally wrecked—and one still pinned beneath the truck's trailer. Apart from a few oil spills that had been covered with sand, piles of shattered glass and vehicle parts lay all over the place. Dozens of boxes and goods that had exploded and scattered everywhere were still being swept onto the side of the road—to clear the way for traffic. By the looks of it, the accident appeared far worse than he had thought. A faint voice in the back of his head whispered that it could've just as easily been him. But he brushed the thought away, concluding that the timing was off. Or was it?

IT WAS ALMOST MIDNIGHT WHEN LENNY'S CAR FINALLY approached Wilmington. The port city was quiet with not a single soul in sight—at least not where he was. *Great! Now whom do I ask for directions?* He slowly rolled the car down the main street, stopping every now and then to scan for an open store or restaurant. But everything was already shut for the night. He thought of looking for a city map. Most visitor and information centers would have them somewhere out front. It was a smart move because less than ten minutes later he had followed the public direction posts and found the large map erected outside a quaint Georgian house in the middle of the Historic Downtown District. He parked the car slightly over the pavement and directed the car's headlights onto the map. It didn't take much time at all to find Turtle Cove. Marked with a picture of a turtle next to the title and a line leading to a brief caption along the side of the map, it showed the distance and the approximate traveling time—twenty-five minutes.

CHAPTER NINE

C arrie's legs were shaking beneath her body. Not from the cold, but in fear. She had briefly looked back a moment ago and he had increased his pace too. *Who is he and why is he following me?* By now she had increased her gait so that she was moving in a light jog. The park was empty—they had closed it off until the ceremony. She kept her eyes on the street up ahead where visitors had started gathering at the market. With her clipboard pinned in the crook of her arm, she glanced back once more. She had to know how far behind her he was. But the man was no longer there. Relieved, she settled back into a brisk walk. She turned her entire body around so she could have a better look, make sure he was gone. Her eyes scanned the park behind her. Nothing. He was gone. She let out a nervous giggle. *Silly woman. You got yourself in a tizzy over nothing.*

When she stepped out into the street she smoothed her hair, drew in a deep breath, and let it out slowly—gathering herself. She willed her red lips into a smile and set off to Al's Hardware.

"You come as if you were called," Al said from behind the counter as soon as she stepped inside.

"Really? Great timing then I suppose," she smiled. "How are we doing with the lanterns?"

"Well, that's kinda what I needed to talk to you about. I've hit a slight snag. The consignment of battery-operated lanterns never arrived—apparently, the truck overturned on the way here. They won't have another truck heading this way until next week."

"Oh, that's not good. Any chance any of the nearby towns' hardware stores might loan us some?"

"I've already checked. They don't have spares."

Carrie fell silent as she thought her way through the problem. She checked the time on her watch.

"Okay, we still have a little bit of time. I'll have Betty quickly put together a craft table—we'll offer free DIY paper lanterns. She should know how to make them. It's a fire hazard but we'll make sure everyone follows the necessary safety rules. I'll get Chief Perry to stand by with a firetruck just in case." She scribbled on her notepad.

"You're a genius, Carrie Claiborne. This town is so blessed to have you, you know that?"

"Aw, thanks, Al. Only doing what any mayor's wife would do." She flashed a smile and left.

As she made her way towards the Crafting Queen craft shop, she reached for her mobile to make a call to Chief Perry. As she dialed his number she noticed her battery showed four percent. She'd forgotten to charge it earlier. Taking the chance she made the call anyway. The chief didn't take long to answer so she quickly filled him in. The battery died the second she ended the call.

THE CRAFT SHOP WASN'T ON THE MAIN ROAD. IT WAS AT the end of a short lane one block down. She'd have to hurry before Betty finished her last workshop for the day. Once she was done, she'd quickly swing by the house to pick up her portable phone charger then make her way down to the tree for the switching-on ceremony. When she rounded the corner at the end of the block she pulled her coat's collar higher over her neck as the icy wind hit her face. The alley was dark and empty. She realized the Christmas parade had already started— everyone would by now have made their way to the other side of town. Please let her be there, she prayed.

Her heels noisily hit the cobbled lane, sending

echoes into the chilly evening air. She pinned her eyes on the small shop. From where she was she could already tell the shop had closed. She briefly stopped, contemplating whether to even bother going closer. As the noise of her shoes died down, she heard a second set of footsteps somewhere behind her. She spun around. Peered into the darkness. Listened. There was no one there. She turned and carried on toward the shop about ten yards away—just to be certain. When she got to the door she jiggled the knob. It was locked. She put her face between her hands on the window and peered inside. The shop was deserted. As she stood still in front of the shop at the end of the lane, she heard footsteps again. Perhaps Betty had come back. Perhaps Al got to her first.

"Hello? Betty, is that you?" she called into the darkness. Her back was pinned up against the shop's door in fear. No one answered. She strained her eyes to see better in the shadows. But saw nothing. She waited, listened. She thought she heard a shuffle halfway down the lane. Her heart pounded noisily against her chest. Her throat went dry.

"Hello? Who's there?" she called out again. This time with a slight quiver in her voice.

Her insides lay in a knot in the pit of her stomach. *Run!* her instincts told her. But she was trapped in the alley. There was nowhere to run but back down the lane. Toward the noise.

With her back still pinned against the door, she fixed

her eyes on the dark lane in front of her. Her hand blindly searched for the door handle behind her back. When she found it she jiggled it again, this time with more force. The door didn't budge. She thought of breaking the window in the door with her elbow—like the burglars did on the tv shows. Once inside she could use the phone to call the police. But what if she was just paranoid? Broke Betty's window for nothing. Fearful for no reason like in the park earlier.

She decided she'd brave the walk back down the alley instead. After all, whatever she'd heard was no longer there. *Probably a rat.* She made a mental note to contact the council about it in the morning.

She slowly pushed herself away from the door. Took one small step, then one more. Slowly, quietly, on full alert. Her heart pulsed noisily in her ears. Her body went rigid. She paused, listened, nothing. Two more steps. This time she moved faster. When nothing happened she increased her stride, strained her ears. She felt like crying. She felt like throwing up. *Pull yourself together, woman. Your mind's running away with you.* She pinched her eyes closed, took a deep breath, and let it out slowly. She shook her hair back as if to shake the fear away and set off down the dark alley toward the quiet street. From inside the recessed doorway of another shop directly to her right, something moved in the shadows. Her body jerked to a halt. Then she saw him. The man from the park.

MAYOR GRAYSON CLAIBORNE SCOOPED HIS LITTLE GIRL up in his arms as she darted away from Adam toward him.

"Fly me, Daddy. Fly me! I'm an angel."

"You're getting too old for me to pick you up, Maribelle," he laughed. "Even though you're the most beautiful angel I've ever laid eyes on."

He kissed her forehead and lowered her to the ground.

"Now where's that other angel of mine, huh?" he asked Adam, referring to Carrie.

"I'm sure she's flying around here somewhere. We'd agreed on meeting back here for the ceremony. Although she should've been here already, we're about to start," Adam said.

"Knowing that wife of mine she's probably taking care of a tiny emergency somewhere. She won't be happy until everything is perfect." Grayson turned his attention to his daughter. "So how about you and I let Pastor Adam do his thing and we go find ourselves a lantern?"

"I'm singing, Daddy, in the angel choir. See?" Maribelle pointed to where the carolers had already lined up in front of the tall Christmas tree.

"Sorry, Grayson, thought you knew. It was a last-minute thing to help Carrie out. She looked a bit overwhelmed with everything so I kinda created the opportunity to give her a little space."

"Nothing to be sorry for, Adam. Thank you, that was a very considerate gesture. I'm sure she'll surface any second now. Go on then, little angel. Go sing your heart out."

Grayson waited until Maribelle joined the choir, excused himself, then dialed Carrie's number from his mobile. It went straight to voicemail. He dialed it again. It made no difference. Something left him unsettled. It wasn't like Carrie not to have her phone on. He dialed it once more. Still he got the same result. Being almost six foot five, Grayson towered over most people. So he stood in place and scanned his eyes over the crowd, turning slowly in a circle. But with the glow from the dozens of lanterns, it was hard to see anyone's face clearly. He asked Adam, who was now in conversation with a member of his team, to keep an eye on Maribelle and to call him when Carrie got there—just in case he missed her.

He moved through the crowd asking along the way if anyone might have seen his wife. No one had, except Al who told him she had left his store to go to Crafting Queen.

"But that was ages ago, Mayor. Funny thing is, she never did get to speak to Betty. I happened to bump into her over at the games table and we got to work on the lanterns straight away," Al reported.

Grayson thanked Al and stood to one side. He checked the time—it was five minutes to midnight. In the background he heard the carolers singing. Perhaps he'd missed her. He dialed Adam's cell.

"No, she's still not here, Grayson. This isn't like her. She's never late," Adam said.

"I know. Something must be wrong. I'm going to pop in at the house. Maybe she's there. Call me if you see her."

"Will do."

"And, Adam, please keep her in your prayers. I don't want to assume the worst, but I can't shake this feeling that she's in trouble."

"Will do, but I'm trusting she's around here somewhere. She has to be."

CHAPTER TEN

As Grayson walked away from the crowd he heard the countdown to the switching on of the Christmas tree lights. In the nearly twelve years they had lived in Turtle Cove, Carrie had never once missed the opening of any of the town's events. She took her role far too seriously for that. His long legs pushed faster across the park's lawns and on to the road, frustrated that he didn't have his car. He had walked the three blocks from his house to free up parking for the visitors. Now he wished he hadn't. His body went cold at the thought that something might have happened to his wife. It left his insides roiling with fear. *Fear not, for I am with you; be not dismayed, for I am your God...* the words of one of his favorite verses in Isaiah dropped into his head. Instantly he felt convicted. He whispered a prayer for forgiveness and asked God to strengthen him, help him, let Carrie be safe.

But when he eventually burst through their home's front door, the house was quiet. He called for her. No answer. Upstairs their bedroom was empty, as was the office. There was nothing to indicate that she had been back there since that morning when they had both left home together. His stomach did a somersault. His heart pulsed out of control.

He dialed her mobile again. Still no answer. This time he left a message on her voicemail. *The Crafting Queen!* He was reminded that Al had said she'd gone there to find Betty. But he'd seen Betty at the tree and she had confirmed that she never saw Carrie. His mind raced through possible scenarios, avoiding a few that made his blood run cold with fear. He dared not think the worst. He wouldn't.

He was going to go back to the ceremony to see if she, in the interim, might have made her way back there, but as he moved toward the front door, he changed his mind. He'd go look for her at the craft shop—just in case. With his body now flushed with adrenaline, he slammed the front door too hard on his way out and the fresh Christmas wreath fell to the floor behind him. The glass ornaments shattered into a million pieces on the porch. That would usually upset Carrie, but right now he'd let her go off at him. He just wanted her safe. He reminded himself to be strong and remain in faith. For a brief moment, hope filled his heart. Perhaps she accidentally got locked inside the shop. It was a stupid thought, he knew, and it didn't make any sense, but he was desperate to cling to something. He leaped over the three porch steps toward the driveway. This time, he would take his car.

When Grayson neared the alley he almost rammed his car into the bollards at the start of the lane. He left his car running and set his headlights on full.

"Carrie! Are you here?" he called out as he ran up toward the craft shop at the farthest end of the lane. She didn't answer. With his eyes fixed only on the shop's door and windows, he didn't see it. He knocked on the door, jiggled the handle. No answer. Inside, the shop was dark. She wasn't there. It was only when he turned around, his hands folded in hopelessness and frustration on top of his head, that his eyes finally spotted it.

At first, his legs didn't want to move. Perhaps his mind hadn't fully comprehended yet what his eyes were telling him. Then, as if an invisible hand had shoved him forward, he leaped toward it.

In the dark shadows just beyond the light of his car, he found Carrie's clipboard. He stooped to pick it up. The pages were dirty, bent and torn in places. Something his wife would've never let happen.

"Carrie!" his voice echoed through the darkness, his eyes frantically searching every nook and cranny of the lane.

Inside, his body couldn't fully process the raging emotions that flooded his every cell. Fear, anger, hopelessness, sadness overwhelmed him all at once.

"Carrie!" he yelled once more as he ran back toward his car. But she was nowhere in sight. "Carrie!"

In a desperate attempt—or perhaps it was denial—he dialed her phone once more. Again it went straight to voicemail. From the corner of his eye, trapped beneath one of his car's wheels, he spotted a black, leather glove. Please don't let it be hers! Please! he pleaded silently as he hurriedly rolled his car back. But when he went to pick it up and held it in his large hands, he saw the small gold insignia with her initials on the cuff and knew without a shadow of a doubt, that the single glove belonged to his wife.

LENNY PUSHED HIS CAR ALONG THE WINDING COASTAL road until he passed the sign that welcomed him to Turtle Cove. Unlike the reception he'd received when he arrived in Wilmington, Turtle Cove was very much alive and bursting with energy. Rows and rows of parked cars lined the short winding coastal road as soon as he entered the town. Festive music blasted through the car's windows. Above his head, the entire street was decorated with arching Christmas scenes which lit up the entire town. In the far distance, he saw illuminated market stalls and heard the loud cheers of people participating in a few festive gaming activities, and a small rowdy bunch of kids in a Santa's Workshop play area. He had never experienced anything like it.

He decided to park his car and walk to where he saw the large Christmas tree drenched in the most captivating lights and decorations. Around it, a small crowd was gathered singing Christmas carols. As he neared the area he couldn't help but feel attracted to it, almost mesmerized by the sincerity, the joy, the peace that emanated from it. He caught himself smiling. As if something deep inside his soul had been woken up. Not even when he had the winning hand against Royal Crush—the reigning underground poker champ who never lost—had he felt excitement. It was as if his soul had finally found the missing link to life—community. He stood there, on the outskirts of the gathering, watching, taking it in. When the carolers finally finished, a man spoke of the king of all kings. The one who came to set us free. He spoke of his love for all, and how his entire birth, every last detail of it, was planned by God. How nothing was accidental, even when there was no room available in the inn. All of it fit into God's plan to bring salvation to the world. Lenny watched the man's face as he spoke. There was a fire in his eyes. A fire that held the crowd captive. A fire that could never be extinguished. Suddenly Lenny longed to have what he had.

Longed to be free. Was this why Carrie chose to live there?

The reminder of his sister jolted his heart into the present. He started scanning the crowd's faces, slowly moving between the people. But she was nowhere to be found. Fear squeezed at his insides. Fear that he might be too late. And as he was once again reminded of the mess he had made of his life, the man with the fire in his eyes spoke again.

"Amazing how God works stuff out in His time when the worst looks like the best there is. Sometimes it takes a lifetime of bad things to happen to recognize the goodness of God."

Once again Lenny found himself pinned to the spot, digesting the man's words. It was only when a loud voice shouted Carrie's name from the back of the crowd that Lenny snapped out of his daze.

"Carrie! Has anyone seen my wife? Carrie!" Grayson yelled as he pushed between his townsfolk.

Quiet murmurs among the people ensued as he made his way to the front. Begging for anyone to say they'd seen her. But one by one they announced they hadn't seen her since earlier in the evening. When he finally made it to the front, he whispered into the preacher's ear, and Lenny watched as the fire in his eyes disappeared for the slightest of moments. Then the tall man who knew his sister turned to pick up a little girl. She looked exactly like Carrie had when she was little.

Lenny instantly knew who they were. He pulled out the newspaper clipping he had stuck inside his jacket pocket; darted his eyes back and forth between the photo and the tall man's face. It was him. Carrie's husband. And that was their little girl. His niece.

Lenny's insides churned. At that moment, he knew he was too late. Diaz had gotten to her first. If it wasn't for the overturned truck he would have made it in time. He cursed under his breath. He had failed to protect his sister.

A young woman took the little girl by the hand and they skipped away. When they were out of earshot, the man spoke into the crowd again. This time with more urgency. He told them that he had found her clipboard and glove. Explained where. He begged the crowd for information. Pleaded for them to give him the answers he sought. But none were forthcoming.

Do something, you fool! Tell him!

With trembling legs, Lenny pushed his way through the crowd towards the man and stopped directly facing him.

"Are you Carrie's husband?" he said with as much courage as he could muster.

"Yes, have you seen her?" he said, his eyes suddenly full of hope.

"No. But I know what happened to her."

"What? Where is she?" Grayson dropped down until his eyes were level with Lenny's.

"Tell me!" he urged when Lenny struggled to find the words.

"I'm Lenny, Leonard actually. I'm Carrie's brother."

Grayson went silent and briefly turned to Adam as if he hadn't heard him correctly.

"You're Carrie's brother. The one who went to jail?" Grayson finally dared to ask.

"That was a long time ago, but yes."

Grayson turned away, his hands on his hips, his nostrils flared.

"What have you done this time, huh? What have you done that landed my wife in trouble?" He suddenly turned and shook Lenny by the shoulders.

"Huh? Answer me! What mess have you made this time?"

"Let's just take a moment here, Grayson." Adam pushed himself between the two men.

Grayson stepped back, his hands clasped in his habitual manner on top of his head, pacing back and forth in a small circle.

"Lenny, I'm Adam. Tell us what you know, please? Is she okay?"

CHAPTER ELEVEN

W hen Lenny stared into Adam's eyes, the fire was no longer there. It had been replaced by something else. Something he didn't recognize. It wasn't fear, nor anger nor hope.

"Is she okay, Lenny?" Adam repeated his question.

"I don't know. I don't even know where she is. But these guys… these guys are dangerous. They know people. Very influential people. That's all I know."

"How do you know them and what do they want with Carrie?" Adam asked.

"I got into business with them. I lost something that was theirs and they want it back. They think I took it, but I didn't. I wouldn't. I got robbed. Someone drugged me and took it. But these guys, they don't believe me. So they took Carrie."

"That's absurd! Tell me who they are! Who took

her?" Grayson lost control and was suddenly in Lenny's face again. It scared him. He jumped back two feet.

"I don't know, okay! I'm worried too, you know. She's my sister."

"You were nothing but trouble in her life, Leonard," Grayson said in anger. He instantly regretted his words, but he was too upset to think clearly. Too worried.

"Sorry, I didn't mean that. Just help us find her before…"

Lenny didn't want to hear the words any more than Grayson wanted to speak them.

"We need to call the police," Adam said.

"No! You can't. They'll kill her if I involve the police," Lenny said in a panic. "They'll kill her if they know I'm here talking about them!"

"Well, we've got to do something. We can't just stand here and wait." Grayson was visibly upset, his voice echoing above the murmurs of the small crowd of community members who had stayed nearby.

"I suggest we go to your house, just in case they call with a ransom or something," Adam said.

"There won't be a ransom. They don't want your money. They want—"

Lenny stopped, careful not to give too much away.

"What, Leonard? Talk!" Grayson pushed again.

"They want the package."

"What package?" Adam said.

"Just a package, okay."

"What's *in* the package, Leonard?" Grayson again struggled to maintain his composure.

"I don't know. I have no idea. I collect. I deliver. They pay me. Except this time someone stabbed me in the neck with something and then stole it out from under my nose." He yanked down his collar, flexed his neck, and pointed out the injection mark, feeling the need to prove he wasn't lying.

"Well, how are we supposed to find this package if you don't even know who took it from you? Or what's in it!" Grayson continued.

"I don't know. Not exactly."

"What does that mean? *Not exactly.*" It was Adam's turn to ask and hopefully defuse Grayson's temper in the process.

"There's this girl. She's one of their go-betweens. I think she knows more than she's letting on. I need to get her to talk."

In a flash, Grayson had Lenny by the elbow of his bad arm and turned him in the direction of his car.

"You're hurting me!"

"Where's this girl?" Grayson pushed, ignoring his plea as he steered him away.

"She's back in Atlanta. Let go of my arm. Please! I'll take you there."

"Grayson, wait!" Adam interjected. "You can't just up and leave. You have a responsibility, a reputation. Our entire town will want to know what's going on. Not to mention Maribelle who now needs her father more than ever. People will talk. You need to protect her."

Adam's sensible words gave Grayson sufficient reason to stop. He let go of Lenny's arm, turned away, and rubbed the back of his head.

"I have to do something, Adam," he finally said in a voice laden with emotion.

"I know, Grayson. But we need to properly think this thing through. We have no idea who or what we're dealing with here. One wrong move and Carrie could…" He intentionally didn't finish his sentence.

"We have to call the police. I know people. I'm the blasted mayor for goodness sake!"

"That you cannot do. You can't call the police. I've heard Diaz has connections all over the police force. His clients are some of the most influential people in the entire state of Georgia. Heck, probably the entire country. This man is evil to the core."

Lenny's voice trailed. "Besides, he knows who you are."

"He what? How?" Grayson growled.

Lenny took the crumpled article from his pocket and held it out for Grayson to see.

"This is how he let me know that he was coming here to take Carrie."

"How did he… Who is this man?" Grayson said, his hand behind his neck again.

"I told you. He knows everyone."

"You said his name was Diaz." Adam spoke calmly.

Lenny nodded in reply.

"Is that his first or last name?"

"I only know him as Diaz."

Grayson stared him down.

"That's all I know. I swear."

"What's that?" Grayson had spotted the red-lettered piece of paper sticking out from underneath Lenny's cast.

Lenny shuffled uncomfortably and snuck it back in.

"Nothing."

"It's something all right. I can tell just by the way you're reacting," Grayson pushed.

"It's nothing, okay? It has nothing to do with any of this."

"Take it out," Grayson said in a low, forceful voice.

Lenny ignored him and stood back a few feet.

"Leonard, so help me... You're hiding something. Take it out!"

Before Lenny could react, Grayson's large hand folded around his cast and yanked the piece of paper from its hiding place.

Lenny's face flushed bright red as he watched Grayson scan through the tract. Seconds later he handed it back.

"I'm sorry, Leonard. I don't know what came over me. Sorry. It's this thing with Carrie; I'm not thinking clearly. I just feel so helpless."

Lenny didn't say anything. He quietly pushed the piece of writing back between his cast and wrist.

"Did you find the answer?" Adam asked Lenny.

"To what?"

"To the question."

Lenny knew he was referring to the question on the leaflet. He just shook his head.

"Maybe when all this is over I can tell you. If you haven't found the answer yourself before then, that is."

Lenny nodded.

"I should go," he said. "If I leave now I can be there by sunrise."

Every fiber of Grayson's being wanted to get in that car with Lenny, but he knew Adam was right. Maribelle needed him. And he needed to be home just in case these people made contact. Or Carrie managed to escape.

He turned to Adam, his eyes urgent and begging. He didn't have to say anything. Adam knew exactly what he was thinking.

"Oh, I don't know, Grayson. This is something the police should handle."

"No, I told you! No cops. We will all end up dead!" Lenny said in a panic.

The two men ignored him and Grayson continued.

"Adam, please. You know people too. If things get out of hand you can call them. Besides, I trust you more than anyone else I know."

"Who? What are you talking about? Who can you call? I told you. No—"

"Yeah, yeah calm down. We're not going to call the police. It's too risky. But Adam here has connections who could help," Grayson explained.

Lenny snickered.

"You, connections? I thought you were the preacher. No offense but I don't think the pope's going to be enough to handle these guys."

"It's not the pope, Leonard. Adam's linked to the military. A covert operations unit, to be exact. If we can't go to the police they're our best bet. But we have to do something, Adam. Every second that passes is a second closer to Carrie's death. They could be torturing her as we speak!" The more Grayson spoke the more upset he got.

"They're not going to torture her. They're trying to get me to track down the package. That's all they're interested in. They gave me three days to find it. I came here first to find Carrie, to warn her, to get her to safety. But the stupid truck on the highway... Anyway, it doesn't matter now. I have to get back to Atlanta, find the girl, and make her talk."

"I'll go with him," Adam announced, "and I'll make contact with Gabriel and see what he can find out about this Diaz guy. In the meantime, go pick up your little girl and try to get some rest. I'll keep you posted."

"Thank you, Adam, thank you! Please bring her home. I can't go on without her."

"I know, Grayson. I know."

ADAM HAD OFFERED TO GET BEHIND THE WHEEL ON their drive back to Atlanta. They decided to take his car instead of Lenny's, presuming that by now Diaz and his men might have caught wind of the make of Lenny's car and his whereabouts.

Lenny was asleep the entire time, leaving Adam enough time to make contact with Gabriel—and pray. About thirty miles outside the city, his phone rang. It was Gabriel reporting back on his findings.

"Adam, you might want to sit down for this one," Gabriel warned.

"I'm still in the car. We're not far from the city."

"You're not going to like what you're about to hear."

"Just give it to me straight, Gabriel. What do you know?"

"I'll start with the easy stuff. His full name is Fernando Diaz. Age thirty-two, Brazilian. He came to the US as a child of illegal immigrants. Both his parents were caught, deported back to Brazil. But somehow they had managed to hide Fernando and his younger brother, Carlos. They were left behind, hidden within the pews of a church. He was twelve at the time. They were in and out of foster homes until they finally ran away. They spent the next few years living on the streets of New York. The brother died in nine-eleven. Wrong place, wrong time type of thing. Diaz worked as a janitor at a leading financial firm on Wall Street. Somehow he got into bed with some pretty influential people."

"Tough life," Adam commented. "So, he's still a janitor?"

"If only. Now's where we get to the interesting part. It turns out the guy is a real piece of work. Smart as a tack. He did a little trading of his own."

"Drugs."

"Nope. That would have been too easy for this guy. He's wheeling and dealing in trade secrets."

"Trade secrets, like corporate espionage?"

"And some! This guy's been suspected of financial fraud, money laundering, conspiracy to defraud the United States, Theft of trade secret technology for the Chinese government, Russia, you name it. He's in deep. Real deep."

Adam went quiet.

"You still there?"

"Uh-huh"

"Are you sure you want to do this, Adam?"

"I have to, Gabriel. He's got Carrie. I gave Grayson my word."

"I was hoping you'd say that."

"Why?"

"It seems he makes use of some unorthodox ways to communicate. We're talking secret coded message exchanges. Old-school style. And well, I can't think of anyone better equipped to handle this job than you. MIS has been after this guy for years. The files were classi-fied—highest clearance. I don't want to bring my team in on this. Not yet. Who knows how far his influence stretches? I think the smartest decision would be to keep this as small as we can at this stage. Strictly me and you with a small covert team consisting of a handful of my best guys. We're going to need eyes in the backs of our heads."

"Agreed."

"I've made arrangements for you at a small motel on Peachtree. I'll send you the details. You can trust Tanisha. You'll find a gun in the safe and some cash. Also, I've left a secure mobile phone with tracking. Anything else you need, just shout."

"No guns. I don't want any guns."

"I understand. But, Adam, this guy is a slimy snake. Cool as a cucumber on the outside, but seriously messed up on the inside. There's no telling how far he will go. And once he starts suspecting you're with us, he'll need no excuse to kill you. The gun is just for backup. I'll leave it there in case you change your mind. Once you arrive at the motel, I'll have eyes and ears on you at all times. See what you can get out of the girl and we'll meet up afterward. And make sure you connect the ear piece before you leave the room. At all times. Clear?"

"Got it."

"And, Adam, God be with you."

CHAPTER TWELVE

Carrie's head throbbed as she peeled her body off the floor. She propped herself up into a half-seated position. Suddenly overwhelmed with dizziness and nausea she paused for a moment. Her skin still stung where his hand had struck her cheek. The burning sensation had her thinking about her mother. And that night.

There was nothing but pitch black darkness around her. Sobs threatened to overwhelm her, but she held them back. She needed to stay calm. Her mind ran over what had happened. She recalled the man in the alley's face and how he had accosted her. Why her? What did he want? She had no idea who he was or what he was planning to do with her, but it scared her.

She had tried to avoid being captured. Kicked and fought him off as best she could. But he was too strong.

Thinking back, she'd had no chance against him. And bargaining with him had had no effect either. He had declined her watch and phone when she told him he could take them. Not even a large sum of money interested him. All she could conclude was that someone who had it in for Grayson had kidnapped her.

She found herself quickly thanking God that he took her instead of Maribelle. Had it not been for Adam inventing her role as an angel, her daughter would have been with her in that alley. The thought left her even more grateful to God for being in control.

She dried her eyes with the forearm part of her coat's sleeve and strained her eyes in an effort to see through the pitch-black darkness. It was dead silent. By way of habit, she moved to take off her gloves, pausing as she realized she had lost one. With both hands bare she slid them across the floor to feel her way through the darkness. There was nothing but space. The floor she'd been lying on was carpeted. Not plush carpets. More like those rough stick-on squares they use in cheap office buildings. She blinked several times when black patches blurred her vision.

"Hello?" she called out in a quivering voice.

Nothing. Again her emotions threatened to get the better of her. To the point where her entire body trembled. *Lord keep me calm!*

She inhaled, held it for a second or two then slowly exhaled. Her mind took her to a conversation she'd once had with one of the visually impaired children at the hospital during a charity event in Charleston. The boy had told her that his other senses compensated for his loss of sight. Being blind sharpened them. She shut her eyes tight and allowed her senses to adjust. Almost instantly she heard a whirring sound coming from somewhere behind her. She turned an ear toward it. It sounded like a ceiling fan. She remained still, listening, honing her senses. A faint knocking sound drew her attention to the opposite end of the room. She recognized it. It sounded like a tilt wand knocking against the slats of a Venetian blind. The metal ones. *A window!*

The prospect of escaping excited her and she instantly moved onto her hands and knees. Gently crawling on all fours she made her way toward the slow tapping sound. It didn't take long before her shoulder hit something hard and she winced. Whatever it was moved with the impact. Her hands followed the shape and settled on the flat surface above her head. It was a table. She sat back on her knees and stretched her hands across the tabletop, knocking something to the floor in the process. It made a small thudding sound on the floor and stopped next to her knees. She reached for it, determining the shape of a coffee mug. Her heart pounded excitedly against her chest. *It's a desk. I'm in an office.* She opened her eyes again for the first time but quickly shut them again when the black patches returned. As she traced the outlines of the desk she pulled herself up against it and carefully glided her hands across the multitude of papers that lay scattered all over the desk. There was a cup with pens, a stapler, and a clipboard of sorts. She was hoping, praying, for a desk lamp. Soon after her prayers were answered. When she found a sticky metal lamp in the corner on the far end of the wooden desk her fingers clumsily followed the cord to find the switch. As she lay hands on it she drew in a sharp breath in anticipation. She flipped the switch. Nothing. She flipped it again, on and off, still nothing. A faint whimper escaped from her lips but she swiftly refocused her mind. Her hands followed the cord down to the floor and she crawled alongside it to where it eventually stopped.

"No, no, no!" she cried softly when her hands felt the familiar outlines of the power plug that lay free on the floor. Tears threatened behind her closed eyelids.

Find the outlet, Carrie. Don't give up.

As she crawled across the floor, one hand outstretched, reaching forward in search of the wall, she felt nothing but emptiness. She sat up on her knees, her legs folded beneath her. Again she listened. Should she abandon the search for the power outlet and go back to finding the window? She brushed her hair from her face and decided to try once more—three feet in each direction. Excitement rushed through her when her fingers finally hit the wall. With one hand she held onto the plug and cord while the other scrabbled along the wall until she found the outlet. It took several attempts to line the pins up with the holes in the socket. She tried to stay calm but the will to have her sight back became more urgent by the second, leaving her hands to anxiously fumble with the task. When she finally got it right she worked her way up the cord toward the desk again.

Until her fingers finally flipped the switch and a soft glow surrounded her.

SHE SWUNG AROUND TO TAKE IN THE ROOM. IT WAS small; rectangular in shape, with wood-paneled walls all round. The desk stood in the middle of the floor at one end of the room. It was an office, a construction site office—if she had to take a guess. She made for the door, pressing her ear against it first. It was quiet outside. Her heart pounded hard in her ears. Could it be this easy to escape?

She turned the filthy brass knob. The door was locked. Her heart dropped. She tried again, this time with more vigor while she gently shoved her shoulder against it. The result was the same. There was an empty keyhole. Her eyes scanned the walls on either side of the door for a key, then the desk. But she didn't find anything. On the opposite end, the whirring sound she'd heard earlier was from an air vent—the square box kind that sat inside the wall. She moved to the window and slowly separated two dusty slats with her thumb and forefinger. It was dark outside and there wasn't a single light in sight anywhere. Twisting the wand to open the slats, she peered out into the darkness. There didn't appear to be anyone on guard, not even a dog. Deciding to risk it she pulled the blinds up and pushed the window latch. It didn't move. Upon closer inspection she saw that it had been welded together, intentionally shut. She dashed back to the desk in search of something to break the window with. Apart from the lamp and a derelict office chair, there was nothing else. Deciding it was her only option, she picked up the chair and lifted it onto her hip. It was heavy and she felt clumsy and weak. The first thrust against the window pane made no impact at all. The chair dropped noisily to the floor. Out of breath, she went for it again, swinging it this time like one would when playing baseball. It took every ounce of muscle power in her weak body. But it worked.

Glass shattered noisily to the floor. The chair's legs wedged between the glass and the frame of the window. She yanked it out, nearly falling back onto her rear, then propped it beneath the window. She needed to be quick now—just in case someone had heard the racket. From her position on top of the chair, she swung her legs over and out the window, one by one, then thumped the six feet down to the ground below.

Her body ached all over and blood gushed from one of her hands where the glass had sliced her palm open.

She pushed her palm down onto her other arm, using the fabric of her coat to absorb the blood. The night air was icy cold, the ground beneath her wet and muddy. She pushed herself up and started running. Where to, she had no idea. She just ran. The moon was full but partly hidden behind stormy clouds. It cast dark shadows in front of her. She wanted to cry—out of fear or joy, she wasn't sure. Beneath her unsteady feet, the earth gave way in places where the rain had left potholes. She fell and nearly broke her ankle. The situation forced her to pause and take a look at her surroundings. In places where the clouds had allowed for the area to be illuminated, she could tell it was a construction site of some kind. A few large construction vehicles were parked between large mounds of dirt and boulders—as if they'd been switched off midway between loads—as was also the case with the two diggers behind them. She thought of using one of the trucks to escape but quickly dismissed the farfetched idea that she'd have the sense to know how to drive one.

Once again back on her feet, she decided to keep running. And it wasn't long before she saw them. Train tracks.

CHAPTER THIRTEEN

The roadside hotel was unassuming and falling apart in places. Situated on the lower end of Peachtree Road, it was just after sunrise when they pulled into the small parking area. It had started to rain hard. Large drops pelted down on the car's windows. Lenny was still asleep.

"Hey, Lenny, wake up. We're here."

"I'm up, I'm up!" he said, startled into an upright position.

"Wait here."

Adam pulled the hood of his navy coat over his head and made a run for the reception office. A flickering neon orange sign in the window told him to pull the door open—not push. Once inside he was greeted with a stern look by a woman who reminded him of his history teacher from school. She was African American with short red-brown hair—a wig. In front of each ear from which enormous gold hoop earrings dangled past her chin, her hair smoothed down into two pointy tails. She wore bright peach-colored lipstick that perfectly matched her overly peachy cheeks which in turn also matched her long fingernails. Slightly on the fuller side, her dark green velvet pantsuit seemed to sit far too tight to convince him that she was comfortable in it. As Adam stepped into the building, her huge black eyes peered out from beneath a pair of frameless glasses that balanced on her nose.

"Wipe your feet."

Adam suddenly felt like a child again.

"Of course, ma'am, sorry."

He stepped back to wipe his feet on the large welcome mat. She looked him up and down.

"Where's Lenny?"

"He's in the car," Adam answered, surprised that she knew their names. *It's supposed to be covert?*

"It is."

"What?"

"Covert."

"How did you—"

"I've been doing this a very long time, honey. There ain't nothing that slips past Tanisha. Besides, your eyes are an open book. You might want to control that. Here, I was told to give you this." She handed him a yellow envelope. "Don't open this until you're in the room.

Then leave it under your mattress when you're done. Everything else you need is in your room already. It's the one on the corner at the far end, number sixteen. You can park your car in the space directly in front of it."

She handed him the room key, placed one hand on top of the other, and stared at him over the top of her glasses, her eyes telling him to leave—the same scornful look Adam used to get in school when he was late for class.

He briefly thanked her and dashed back to the car.

"Why does it look like you've just come out of the headmaster's office?" Lenny commented as Adam dropped into the driver's seat.

"Because I feel like I just did. Tanisha's a tough one. You might want to stay on her good side."

"Did she happen to say anything about food? I'm starving."

"Nope, and I'm not going back in there to ask her about it either. We'll freshen up and find something on our way to the girl."

"What time is it?"

"Nearly six."

"We're too early. She only opens her stand around seven. It's about ten minutes from here."

"Timing's perfect then," Adam said as he opened the door to their room.

In total contrast to the motel's modest exterior, their

room was surprisingly spacious and luxurious. There were two comfortable twin beds with fresh white linen, a dark brown leather couch, and a small eating area. To their right was an attached bathroom with fluffy white towels and a few essential toiletries.

Lenny let out a long breathy whistle of surprise before he flopped down onto one of the beds.

"Knock me over with a feather. This place is rocking. I might never want to leave," he said.

Adam didn't comment. Deep in thought, he dropped his overnight bag atop his bed and took a seat at the small table. His fingers fumbled with the seal on the back of the yellow envelope. He was nervous. He'd never taken on anything as dangerous as this. He shut his eyes briefly and exhaled slowly, puffing up his cheeks as he did so. He emptied the contents of the envelope on the table in front of him.

"What's that?" Lenny asked as he watched him from his bed.

"Everything they have on your friend, Diaz."

"He's not my friend. And who's 'they'?"

Adam closed the folder and looked up at Lenny to search his face.

"Are you one of them, Lenny? Can you be trusted?"

Adam's question caught Lenny by surprise.

"You're joking, right?"

Adam shook his head, waiting for an answer.

"No, I'm not! She's my sister, or have you forgotten

that? I don't want to see her killed any more than you do. What do you take me for, huh?"

Lenny was visibly upset. His eyes displaying the sincerity and truth Adam was looking for.

"Fine, I believe you. You strike me as an honest man, Lenny. I don't know your background, but I've been in the people-business long enough to know you've been dealt a rough hand. And so I'm choosing to trust you. Because I think you have a good heart. *And you're searching.* The people of Turtle Cove raised me. They took me in after both my parents were killed in a car crash when I was twelve. They're my family. Grayson, Carrie, all of them. They're all I've got."

He briefly looked down at the folder on the table and then continued. The tone of his voice had changed.

"A few years back, I lost my wife and little girl at the hands of a psychopath. I lost my reason to live, my purpose, my identity. So I set off on a journey to discover the truth about myself and my parents. I'll spare you the details, but, as it turned out my father was a codebreaker for the military. The US Military Intelligence Service, to be exact. You see, my father had this gift for breaking codes, deciphering cryptic messages that were exchanged between hostile countries. Apparently, he was quite good at it too. Good enough to have paid for it with his life. What I didn't realize was that during the twelve years they had raised me, my father taught me everything he knew."

"So you're a codebreaker, not a preacher."

Adam laughed.

"No, not quite. I'm still a pastor, but I help them out every now and then. Long story short, as it happens, MIS has been after Diaz for years. He's a very dangerous man."

Lenny swung his legs over his bed and sat down in the chair opposite Adam.

"So this is Diaz's file?"

"Yep, everything they have on him."

Adam flipped the folder open. A large color photo stared back at them.

"That's him! That's Diaz," Lenny yelled out, suddenly looking very anxious.

Adam filled Lenny in on everything Gabriel had told him over the phone, confirming it with the records that were included in the file—and learning about a few more interesting character flaws in the man.

When he had finished, Lenny suddenly jumped up and started pacing back and forth.

"This guy is dangerous, Adam. I don't know if I can do this."

"We have no choice, Lenny. Not if we want to see Carrie alive again."

Lenny retook his seat, leaning across the small table, his eyes locked with Adam's.

"I never meant for this to happen, Adam. You have to believe me. All my life I've looked out for Carrie.

Took the beatings to protect her. Helped her make something of her life. Somehow I just got left behind and stuck in this world of misfortune. I've been trying to get out for years. I owe a lot of money to a lot of people. This was my only way out. It was supposed to be easy. I was going to pay off my bookies and then live a simple life in Mexico. I have my ticket booked and everything."

He slammed his hand down hard on the table and noisily pushed his chair back roughly so it tipped over on the floor.

"Why does nothing ever go right for me, huh? I had it all planned out. Every time I think, now I'm going to be free, I somehow create an even bigger mess for myself. This one being the biggest mess of all. Trouble finds me no matter how hard I try to make something of my life."

Adam, who had been quietly listening to another five minutes of Lenny's emotional outcry, finally spoke.

"Sometimes we have to go through the desert before we get to the Promised Land."

His words left Lenny frozen to the spot. As if something had drained the very life out of him. With dazed eyes, he spoke in a shaky voice.

"That's the exact thing the drifter in the subway said to me. How did you—why did you say that?"

"Have you ever heard the story in the Bible about the Promised Land, Lenny?"

The way Lenny shuffled uncomfortably told Adam he hadn't.

"God freed the Israelites from hundreds of years of slavery in Egypt. He promised to deliver them to a land of plenty. All they had to do was trust him. But they didn't. When their timeline didn't meet God's timeline, they decided to take matters into their own hands. They set off in search of their utopia on their own, tried to take shortcuts, turned to false gods and idols, and turned their backs on God. It took them forty years wandering through the desert, enduring trial after trial, on the chance that they'd get to the Promised Land. You see, Lenny, their plan didn't align with God's plan for them. God's plan was for them to stay where they were and to help prosper the nation that enslaved them first. But even though they were obstinate and disobedient, God showed them grace. He fed them heavenly bread when they were starving, protected them from enemies, and eventually made good on his promise. Often God's timeline and plan veer away from how we want a situation to play out or an outcome in our favor, but his plans for us always turn out for good. All these trials and hardships we go through are God's way of teaching us along the way, showing us that we can trust him and depend on him. If we choose to accept it. Perhaps the answer has been right in front of you all this time, Lenny."

Adam lowered his eyes to the piece of writing

tucked inside the cast on Lenny's broken arm. Lenny's eyes followed but he didn't say a word.

"Just some food for thought, my friend. Speaking of which, let's plug these earpieces in and go grab something to eat before we head out to find the girl."

CHAPTER FOURTEEN

Lenny barely spoke a word after they left the motel. And Adam didn't push him either. He knew their talk would be a lot for Lenny to digest. Instead, he quietly prayed for God to guide him, protect them, help them see his plan.

When they finally got to the newsstand where Lenny had collected the disposable phone, the small square was bustling with employees on their way to work.

"We should wait until they leave and she's not so busy," Lenny suggested.

"Agreed. Gabriel, can you hear us?" Adam spoke into his high-tech earpiece.

"Affirmative, Adam. We have eyes on you too."

"Oh great! Nothing like pressure," Lenny responded sarcastically, the nerves evident in his voice. "Let's hope we can get her to talk. Maybe we should offer her money. Ask your guy how much we can offer her," he whispered.

"We're not going to offer her money, Lenny. She'll talk. And Gabriel can hear you even if you whisper." He teasingly whispered the last bit.

"No way. She's dead if Diaz finds out. I'm telling you, Preacher, we're going to need to bribe her."

"We'll figure it out. Just do whatever it is you're supposed to do when you're picking up a job and let's take it from there. And stay calm, okay, Lenny? You've got this."

Another five minutes went by before the last of the workforce got their newspapers and the newsstand was clear to approach.

"Here we go. Ready?"

"Uh-huh."

"Take a deep breath and stay calm."

Lenny nodded as the pair closed in on the stand. When they stepped up to the window the girl had her back to them while she was digging in her backpack on the floor. When she turned around, she nearly choked on the fresh piece of gum she had just popped in her mouth.

Her eyes lingered on Lenny's face, then darted to Adam's. She didn't speak.

"It's a great day for a picnic, isn't it?" Lenny said the code phrase.

Still she didn't answer.

Lenny cleared his throat and started repeating the phrase. She interrupted him mid-sentence.

"Well, well, if it isn't my strawberries and champagne guy. I can't believe you're still breathing. Who's he?"

"Alive and kicking. He's a colleague. We need to talk."

"Take your paper and leave. I don't have anything to say."

"I need your help."

"I can't help you."

"Please, he's got my sister."

She clicked her tongue and rolled her eyes.

"I told you you were insane to take on that job."

"Yeah, about that, that's what I want to talk to you about. Tell me what you know."

"I ain't telling you jack, man. I happen to love my life."

"Who was the package for? What was in it? Please! Tell me something, anything. Diaz has my sister and he's going to kill her if I don't get the package back in the next two days."

"You lost it? Sheesh man, you really are stupid."

"Tell me something I don't know, okay! And I didn't lose it. Someone drugged me and stole it. So here I am, looking for answers from you. Why did they steal it? Who would do that? Please, help me."

Lenny was desperate and his voice was low and pleading.

"I can't help you."

"Yes, you can. You just won't. Look, I won't tell him you told me anything, okay? Just tell me *something*. Anything that might help me track it down. My sister's life is at stake, darn it! She has a little girl, a family."

Something in his eyes must have hit a nerve with her. She paused, her eyes lingering on Lenny's face.

"Look, all I can do is give you what the last guy had on him when he died."

"The last guy?"

"Yes, the one who tried his hand at this before you. Unfortunately, he wasn't as lucky as you and didn't live through it."

Something in her eyes had changed when she said that. She ducked below the small counter and popped up a minute later with a bloodstained newspaper that she discreetly slipped into a paper bag.

"Check the classifieds."

"Ha ha, very funny. I'm not looking for a job."

"No idiot. There's a message somewhere in the classifieds. That's all I know. And you didn't get that paper from me, got it?"

"Okay. And you know about a message how?"

The girl gave a burdened sigh.

"He was my boyfriend. The guy before you. I found

this hidden in our apartment a month after they killed him. No one knows I had it, so keep it that way."

"I will, I promise. Thank you."

As Adam and Lenny turned to walk away she added, "It will be a great day for a picnic when you bring the house down. Maybe the sun will shine for me again."

Her words made Adam speak for the first time.

"God willing, we will. Thank you for your help."

"I can't believe our luck! Who knew she had this?" Lenny exclaimed as they walked back to the motel.

"You really think it was luck? How do you figure that?"

Lenny shrugged his shoulders.

"I don't know. I mean think about it. What are the odds she'd been holding onto a paper that has some obscure message in it?"

"I'm guessing you'll say zero."

"Exactly. Pure luck."

"And luck made her change her mind to give it to us?"

"Well, no. Maybe she just felt sorry for me."

"So she felt an emotion."

"Yes, I suppose so."

"So perhaps God stirred her heart, brought her hope at a time she most needed it. Maybe she found that paper as a result of a series of events that happened to her that day. She accidentally dropped something and spotted it under the couch, or decided she'd finally clean the apartment, cleaned out his cupboard after a month of mourning. There could have been a million ways she found that paper and somehow she made a conscious decision to hold onto it. And today, with you, her conscience brought about the decision to give it to you. Luck can't control your mind or your heart, Lenny."

Lenny was quiet.

"So you're saying God planned all of this. Her boyfriend dying and all."

"I'm saying God has a plan for each of our lives. He didn't kill her boyfriend, sinful men did. But he's using the bad event to work out his plan for her life. Whatever that might be. Like a GPS recalculating a route when you've taken a wrong turn. And in the same way, he's working out the plans he has for us. Things don't always go the way we want them to, Lenny. And yes, often-times life kicks us in the shins, but if we understand and trust that God loves us and that it's all part of a bigger plan, he will help us find our way through it."

"I've never thought of it that way."

"People rarely do, my friend. They have to blame someone for the bad stuff that happens in their life. So they blame God. Because they don't know him."

. . .

WHEN ADAM AND LENNY GOT BACK TO THEIR ROOM AT the motel they opened the newspaper to the Classified section and spread it open on the small eating table.

"Okay, what are we looking for?" Lenny asked.

"A coded message."

Lenny watched as Adam grabbed the pen that lay atop a notepad next to his bed. He placed the pen horizontally across the newspaper and slowly glided it up the page and across each ad column.

"I'm not the world's most academic but where I come from you read from the top down. That makes no sense to me. But maybe you clever people have to read from the bottom up."

"I'm not reading. I'm looking for anomalies."

"Sure, I'll go with that," Lenny snickered.

"Look, your mind sequences words together that make sense when you read it in the normal order. That's how its trained. But when you read out of sequence, in this case from the bottom up, your eyes tend to pick out the inconsistencies when it can't make sense of it."

Adam continued through the columns, then suddenly stopped.

"Here, look, a cipher. See there?"

Adam circled the piece of writing that to the naked eye appeared to be a misprint in an ad.

"It's just a bunch of random alphabetic letters."

"This my friend, is a simple Caesar cipher."

"Simple to you perhaps. The only Caesar I know is

the one on the Vegas strip. I was on a roll that weekend."

"Okay, this has nothing to do with gambling. It's a cipher that was used by Julius Caesar to protect military communications between him and his men. It was later used in World War II. The original cipher used by Caesar shifted in threes."

"Like I said, smart people."

"You are smart too, you know. If you know the alphabet, you can decipher this code. Shifting three literally means each letter here was shifted three places in the alphabet. So the letter D becomes A, E becomes B, and so on. When you replace the letters, you have your message."

Lenny watched as Adam worked his way through the code, replacing the letters then copying one letter at a time onto the notepad.

"Well, what's it saying?"

Adam read the message out loud.

"Noon. Bellevue Road. Shoes."

"So it's a secret meeting, a rendezvous."

"Indeed it is."

Adam flipped the paper over to the front page.

"This newspaper is six months old. I guess we missed the meeting."

"Now what?"

"Not sure. Let me think."

A knock at the door startled them both.

"Who is it?"

"Tanisha."

Adam dashed across the room to find Tanisha standing outside the door peering over her glasses.

"Here, it's today's paper. You might want to check for another message." She turned as soon as she pushed the folded newspaper against his chest.

"Uh, okay. Thank you!" he yelled after her.

"Sheesh, Preacher, now I know why you're trying to avoid her. She's not the friendliest, is she?"

"I can hear you, Lenny," Tanisha announced over the ear piece.

Lenny's face drained as he recalled they were under surveillance.

"Not that it's not appealing. I happen to like a little bit of attitude in a woman," he tried to correct his blunder.

"I think you should quit while you're ahead," Adam said amused.

He flattened the daily newspaper onto the table and followed the identical method with his pen. Lenny watched in silence.

"Got it!"

Again he copied the message onto the notepad.

"We have another meeting. Sunset. Warehouse eighty-one. MC two."

CHAPTER FIFTEEN

A dam wasn't sure who out of the two of them was most nervous. But unlike Lenny, he remained calm—at least on the outside. Inside, his nerves were out of control and his stomach had pulled into a tight knot. So much so that he didn't touch the tray of sandwiches Tanisha had brought to their room.

Lenny, on the other hand, devoured most of the platter—evidently, he ate when he was stressed. But truth be told it was nothing more than him currying favor with Tanisha after his previous slip-up.

Tanisha's gourmet platter of sandwiches had nothing to do with catering to their every whim. That was a smokescreen to maintain her cover—"one can never be too careful," she'd said. The real reason she was there was to run them through a safety sequence and to ensure they were well equipped and prepared for any unforeseen incidences at the warehouse.

"Remember, you're not there to confront anyone. Only to gather intel. Stay out of sight at all times. And if anything does happen, use the safe word," she said in a stern voice as she secured a tiny microphone to Lenny's chest.

"So, are you like a secret agent or something?" Lenny asked her.

Tanisha ignored him.

"I'm just asking because I kinda feel like I'm being used for bait or something. Microphones, hidden cameras, what if they catch us?"

"They won't, as long you don't do anything stupid," she said, her voice steely.

"But you're watching my every move though, right? Who's gonna be there for us if things go wrong? Everyone's watching and listening, but who's got our backs, huh?"

"We'll be fine, Lenny. We're not the FBI trying to bust a drug-smuggling ring. We're trying to get Carrie back. Keep that in mind. We'll find someplace safe to hide, find out who's running this meeting and why. That's it. If they have the package, we let Gabriel know and they'll take it from there," Adam assured him.

"Do we even know where this warehouse is?"

Tanisha spread a large city map out on the bed and pointed at the red circle to the east of the city.

"How can you be certain that's the right one? There are a million possibilities scattered all over the city."

"It's the right one," Tanisha said.

Lenny's nerves got the better of him.

"What if you're wrong? Then we've wasted all—"

"It's the right one. We don't make mistakes," she said again.

Lenny raised his arms as if a gun was pointed at him.

"Okay, okay, I'm just saying. I mean who am I to doubt a secret spy?"

He was intentionally mocking her and she knew it. The look in her eyes told him she wasn't impressed.

Adam, who had been quietly poring over the coded message in that day's paper, looked pensive. He had gone through several more backdated newspapers and found further clues. Something nagged at him. Something he just couldn't put his finger on.

"What are you so deep in thought over, Preacher?"

Adam didn't answer. His mind was trying to work through the problem.

Tanisha moved to stand next to him, her arms folded at her waist as if she was waiting for him to give her something.

"If there's something on your mind best to say it," she urged.

He stared back at her, his mind still with the newspaper in front of him.

"I'm just puzzled by the clues. They're not the same. In fact, I went through a few more papers, some dating back as far as a year, and in each one there's a different tail clue."

"I'm listening."

"The message tells them where and when to meet, that's obvious, but what do these last bits mean? They're totally unrelated. Look here: prospect, shoes, M C two, triple long…what's up with that?"

"Good question," Tanisha said. "Gabriel?" she spoke into the air.

"I'm working on it. For now, proceed and see what you can gather."

"Affirmative," she replied.

"Okay, seriously, I feel like I'm that guy from *Mission Impossible* with all this spy talk. Do I also get a gun?" Lenny's enthusiasm was evident.

Tanisha's eyes were quick to let him know the answer.

He didn't push back.

"No guns, no weapons of any kind," Adam added. "And, Lenny, we're not spies or agents of any kind. Don't go thinking you are and land us in trouble. Got it?"

Lenny responded with a mocking salute.

. . .

ADAM AND LENNY ARRIVED AT THE LOCATION AN HOUR before sunset. The warehouse wasn't what they had expected at all. Instead of it being a remote storage facility or manufacturing plant, it was a nightclub on the outskirts of Atlanta.

"I guess these guys do know what they're doing," Lenny commented as they drove by the charcoal building with its name *Warehouse 81* chalked across its wall in luminous pink.

They parked the car on the opposite side of the road, one block up, and made their way to the entrance. As they stepped inside a doorman held up his hand and started patting them down, narrowly missing the hidden microphones that were strapped to their chests.

"It's my buddy's birthday, man. Just here to show him a good time," Lenny said jovially.

Perhaps the false declaration helped because the doorman gave them a nod and let them through.

Since it was too early for their usual nighttime trade, the club wasn't very busy, much to Adam's relief. His eyes caught the empty stage with the three poles lined up on it. Lenny spotted the shocked look on his face.

"I get this isn't quite your thing, Preacher, but don't worry, the girls won't come on until eight. We're likely to get out of here before their routines start."

Lenny was right on the nose. The place left Adam uncomfortable and looking out of place.

They made their way to one of the dark purple, circular fixed seats—one that had a vantage point to most of the other booths. In one of them to their left, a small party of five men were having fun with a scantily clad waitress as she popped down a fresh round of drinks. Adam looked concerned.

"Ah, don't worry, Preacher. Guys like that are harmless. Young and upcoming hotshots out for a quick drink after work. She's used to it. You'd be surprised how well girls like that can handle themselves."

Adam studied Lenny's face.

"Is this a regular thing for you, Lenny? Coming to places like this."

"Not anymore. I won't lie, you being a man of faith and all, but yes, there was once a time when I played a few regular poker games in a club like this one. Their rakes are much lower than the casinos'. Places like these are more often than not a front for a lot of high-stakes poker dens. See that guy over there?" He pointed discreetly to a man dressed in a black shirt and suit, seemingly casually seated next to a red velvet curtain.

"That's the pit manager—the guy who makes sure no one cheats when there's a game in progress. Behind that curtain is where the games take place, but that's much later in the evening."

"I never thought I'd see the day I'm stuck in a place like this," Adam said shuffling uncomfortably.

"You can't bail now, man. Carrie needs us. This is the only lead we have."

"I won't do that, Lenny. But let's face it, it's not as if I'm blending in here. Whoever's going to be at this meeting will spot me from a mile away."

As if Adam couldn't be more uncomfortable the waitress was suddenly next to them.

"What can I get you two handsome lads?"

"A couple of beers thanks, sweetness," Lenny replied with ease.

"Coming right up."

Adam hadn't looked up once. Lenny on the other hand, allowed his eyes to linger on the waitress as she walked away.

"Seriously, Lenny? Get a grip, man. Don't you have any shame?"

"Sorry, Preacher, you're right, I shouldn't be so blatant about it."

It wasn't what Adam had meant but he let it go. He glanced at his watch and scanned the room.

"Gabriel, do you copy?" he said.

"Loud and clear, Adam."

"How long do we sit here?"

But before Gabriel could answer in Adam's ear, Lenny interrupted.

"Apparently not long at all. I have eyes on—"

Lenny froze. He dropped his chin to his chest and quickly popped his hand in front of his face.

"What? Who did you see?" Adam urged showing care not to talk too loudly.

"That's him. That's the guy who drugged me and stole the package," Lenny whispered, his head still bowed.

"You sure?"

"Look at him! Would you forget a guy who looks like that?"

Adam stole a glance. The man was tall, at least six and a half feet, his physique more powerful than any athlete he'd ever seen. And muscular—like the Hulk.

"If he sees me, it's over, Adam," Lenny whispered.

Seconds later the waitress placed two beers and a basket of pretzels in front of them.

"Thank you," Adam said, still not looking at her.

"Okay, we have a job to do. I say we just bear down and get it over with. We need to stay cool, Lenny. You stay here and keep your head down."

"Where are you going? Have you lost your mind?"

Lenny was highly strung.

"I need to get the camera on his face. The lighting's too poor and I don't have a great angle from here. Just stay put."

Adam didn't give Lenny any time to object. He was already on his feet and moving past the table where the man had squashed his enormous frame into one of the booths. When he neared the table, Adam paused directly next to him. Pretending he was looking for signage on the walls, he discreetly angled the camera that was hidden in his coat's button onto the man's face.

"Move on, buddy," the man barked, his voice deep and low.

"Sorry, I was just taking in the decor," Adam said, making sure he kept the camera focused long enough.

"Walk away, man!"

"Fine, fine," Adam replied then hastily made his way back to the table where Lenny, by now, looked like he had a serious case of indigestion.

"Gabriel, did you get that?" Adam asked.

"Affirmative. Great work, Adam. Stand by."

Adam had switched places with Lenny who now sat with his back pinned against the booth's back cushion. He had turned his body sideways too—in a futile attempt to become invisible.

"We should get out of here now while we still can," Lenny whispered from behind the menu that he held in front of his face.

"We have a name," Gabriel announced in their ears. "Meet Jerome Palmer aka The Midget."

"Oh, how original, the man's anything but a dwarf," Lenny snickered as he waited for Gabriel to continue.

"He's been linked to some of the country's most notorious fraudsters, mostly hedge fund fraud, corporate fraud, and cybercrime—no direct involvement it seems. If he is the guy who drugged Lenny, then I suspect he's a runner slash bodyguard. Is he on his own?"

"Yes," Adam said. "No sign of any packages either."

"Let's wait it out. Keep your cover."

Even in the dull red lighting, Adam could see the look on Lenny's face.

"I think it's too late for that," Lenny announced.

CHAPTER SIXTEEN

C arrie's body shivered uncontrollably. Every fiber in her body ached from the cold. Her red coat was drenched in mud and rain from the night before. Frozen half to death, she blew whatever warm air she had left inside her body into her near-purple cupped hands. It had no effect.

The hand that the glass had sliced into had stopped bleeding on its own—presumably from the freezing-cold night.

She had followed the train tracks throughout the night and that entire day, never once stopping. And yet she still found herself in the middle of nowhere with nothing but vast emptiness stretched out all around her. When the man had captured her in the alley he had pulled a hood over her head before he threw her inside the trunk of his car. They had driven for a while but there was no telling how long, or where to. She could be anywhere.

She looked up at the weak sun that was about to set. If she didn't find shelter very soon she would have to spend another night out in the freezing cold. She wasn't sure her body could handle that.

Through purple lips and with a quivering voice she hummed away at the lullaby she'd usually be singing to Maribelle at night. She couldn't remember all the words, she was too cold. But it was what had kept her going this far. She sang the same verse over and over, her voice trailing off as she battled to catch her breath under the cold.

With her eyes fixed on the train track ahead of her, she kept moving—one foot in front of the other. There hadn't been a single train on the line since she'd found it —in any direction. Logic told her it was either abandoned or a route not often used. But it was her only hope. It had to lead somewhere. All her mind needed to focus on now was putting one exhausted leg in front of the other. As long as she kept walking, she should be fine. As long as she kept walking, she would eventually find her way back home to her husband and daughter.

THE BLACK SUBARU PULLED UP OUTSIDE THE MOBILE office on the abandoned construction site. When Diaz

stepped out of the car he immediately spotted the shattered window. He snapped his fingers at two of his men
who promptly rushed toward the office trailer. Moments
later one popped his head out of the window and
announced that the woman had escaped. But Diaz had
already suspected that. By now another one of his men
had started tracking the droplets of blood that trailed
away from the broken window.

"She couldn't have gotten far. Keep looking!" he
shouted after him.

But as Diaz sat next to the small pool of dried blood
on the ground, he knew she'd been gone for some time
already. At least twelve hours, if not longer, for it to
have dried already. He turned facing the direction of the
blood trail, sticking his nose into the air as if trying to
pick up her scent, then suddenly, he spun around and got
behind the wheel of the Subaru.

"Search the perimeter!" he commanded the two
minions near the office.

Diaz slowly pushed the vehicle in the direction of
her escape, picking his tracker up en route. With all four
windows down their eyes scanned across the open
space.

It didn't take him long to hit the railway track.

A quick inspection of the tracks showed more blood;
evidence that he had successfully managed to find her
escape route. He glanced at his watch. The sun was
about to set, and it was predicted the night would push

far below zero degrees. If she was still out there, hiding somewhere, she would never survive the cold. He couldn't risk that. He needed her alive. Or at least for Lenny to think she was still alive.

AS THE LAST OF THE SUN'S RAYS DROPPED BEHIND THE horizon, Carrie was dangerously close to giving up. She had relentlessly been following the railway track that seemed to be never-ending. Nightfall was fast approaching and the temperature had already dropped significantly. She had long since stopped praying. Her faith simply wasn't strong enough. And although she felt guilty for lacking faith, she figured God might forgive her considering her circumstances. But as her body grew weaker by the minute, and the darkness set in, she no longer believed she would survive the horrendous ordeal and get back home to her husband and little girl.

Unable to walk one more step, her legs caved beneath her exhausted body. She collapsed in a heap onto the track. So severe was the cold that it had numbed her to the point where she didn't know if her mind and body were still connected. She didn't even feel the pain when the hard steel bars slammed across her shins and instantly left a massive swelling on each leg. Her limbs seemed to belong to someone else, had a mind of their own that she had no control over. And she battled to stay awake.

But her near slumber state was soon interrupted when humming vibrations pushed up from the steel track beneath her cheek, growing louder and louder by the second. She managed to lift her head, just. By now it was too dark to see anything that far away. Realizing she was sprawled across the train tracks she pushed her body up with as much force as she could muster, and rolled herself off onto the muddy soil alongside it. In the distance, she was certain she saw lights. The tiniest flickers of hope rushed through her frail body. If it was a train surely they would see her. She forced her body off the ground into an upright position and took a few wobbly steps back—for fear of being hit by the train. The lights drew nearer, but the familiar sound of a train hitting the tracks wasn't there. When the lights were almost on top of her, she realized it wasn't a train, but a car. At first, she was excited at the prospect of being rescued. But as her mind made sense of it all, she suddenly realized they had caught up with her.

Adrenaline flooded her frozen veins as she turned and pushed her tired legs as fast as they could go. She didn't dare look back. Across the open plain, her eyes frantically searched for a place to hide. But there was nothing but open, flat dirt in any direction. She heard the roaring of the car's engine, saw the lights bouncing up and down over the ground from the corner of her eye, then her foot slipped on the loose soil, before her ankle twisted sideways, and she hit the ground hard with a loud thud.

Suddenly the man from the alley's voice was right beside her.

"Going anywhere?"

Carrie raised her head, her muddy hair hanging in strings across her face.

"What do you want from me? Just let me go."

She heard him snap his fingers and seconds later two of his men had their large hands in her armpits. They dragged her body toward the black SUV, her eyes fixed on the man's sharp face.

"Let me go, please. I'll give you anything you want. Please!" Her voice had no strength to it. She was pleading, sobbing.

"I don't want you or your money. In fact, you're a thorn in my flesh and quite honestly I don't have the time to babysit you. But, unfortunately, it's the only way I can get your good-for-nothing brother to take me seriously. Your life is in his hands, princess."

The man's words shocked her into submission as they tied her hands together and shoved her into the back of the car.

"No, there has to be some misunderstanding. I haven't seen my brother. I don't even know where he is!" she yelled as he got into the passenger seat in front of her and the vehicle sped off.

"Don't get angry with me, sweetheart. He's the one who got you into this mess."

He checked the time on his watch.

"Don't worry, it should be over very soon. He has about thirty-six hours left to get me what I want."

"And if he doesn't?" she dared.

"Then you both die."

When they got back to the site they shoved her up the steel stepladder and pushed her inside the mobile site office.

"This time nail the door and window shut," he barked.

They forced her down into the corner and dropped a brown paper bag and a blanket on the floor next to her.

"You're no good to me dead so make sure you eat," he said.

The man turned and left her alone on the floor, her hands still tied together with duct tape. Once he had left, she heard his underlings hammer pieces of wood outside the door.

She wasn't sure how long she sat there in the corner crying. Her mind was too busy trying to understand how Lenny had got involved in a mess of this magnitude and why he had to drag her into it too. He had problems with gambling and bookies, but this wasn't that. This man wasn't a bookie. He dressed like a business tycoon.

What had her brother gotten himself into that she had to pay for it with her life?

She hadn't seen or heard from Lenny since the day she visited him in prison. He had told her it was best she didn't come there again, forgot about him, got on with her life. What if her brother didn't care enough to save her life? He could be long gone for all she knew. Run off and left her for dead.

But deep down inside, Carrie knew beyond a shadow of a doubt, that Lenny would never do that to her. He would never turn his back on her. All he had ever wanted for her was a better life. A life their parents weren't prepared to give them. He had covered for her too many times. Protected her, saved her life. No, her brother might have his flaws, and he might have lived his life in a way she knew he'd much rather have preferred not to, but if there was one thing she knew about her brother, it was that Lenny would sooner die for her than have her killed.

CHAPTER SEVENTEEN

The man everyone called The Midget was suddenly towering next to their table. With one swift move, he had picked Lenny up by the scruff of his neck. Feet dangling off the floor, the huge man's nose shoved into his face, Lenny found himself at the mercy of a giant.

"Why are you here?" he demanded menacingly.

"I'm not exactly happy to see you either, you big ape! You stabbed me in my neck. You're a scumbag thief!"

Adam whispered the safe word into his mic, repeating it several times.

"We copy you, Adam. We need you to bait him for more information," Gabriel announced.

Adam wasn't in a position to respond and blow the entire operation. He had also never found himself in a high-conflict situation like this either. His insides squirmed with fear. *What do I do, Father? What do I do?* As brave as he attempted to sound, his words of warning instead sounded feeble.

"Leave my friend alone! We're minding our own business." The Midget ignored him and shook Lenny like a rag doll.

"Unless you've come here looking for a fight with me, you have no business in this club," the big man growled at Lenny again.

"You're my business! I wan't my envelope back!" Lenny didn't back down.

"Not helping here, Leonard!" Adam said as he tried to free Lenny from the man's grip.

The man growled again. Like a lion about to pounce on his prey.

"Keep going, Lenny, you're doing great. We need him to acknowledge the package," Gabriel said.

"Coffee, coffee!" Adam kept yelling out the safe word. "We're going to die here today without coffee!"

The giant man's face turned to Adam, his eyes pensive.

"Who are you talking to?"

"What? No one, the waitress. I'm really desperate for a coffee." He emphasized the safe word.

"What did you do with my package, huh? Why did you steal it?" Lenny tried to distract him.

"You've got company," Gabriel announced in their ears.

Seconds later a posse of five men entered the club. One of them, a short Asian man, approached them. He didn't speak, just looked Jerome Palmer directly in the eyes then walked to the booth where the giant had waited for them earlier. Two of his men followed, the other two stood, arms folded, next to The Midget who then promptly lowered Lenny to his feet.

"Look, guys, we don't want any trouble. We're just here for a good time," Adam tried to defuse the situation.

Over his shoulder, he saw the Asian man beckon his men to bring him and Lenny to their table.

"Oh no, thanks, we're fine here at our table," Adam said quickly. This time to impress upon Gabriel that the situation was getting out of control.

"We need eyes on them, Adam," he instructed.

"I just want a cup of coffee, please?" he said almost whining. But still Gabriel ignored him.

He caught Lenny winking at him. Adam's questioning eyes had no effect on Lenny whatsoever. Instead, he watched as Lenny went at it with the gigantic man again—like David and Goliath.

"Who's he, huh? Your boss? Not such a big man now, are you? You're his dog aren't you, big boy? His puppet!"

Every muscle in Adam's body twitched with annoyance at Lenny's blatant mocking. He warned him off with his eyes, but Lenny ignored him. Again, the kingpin beckoned. Immediately The Midget's enormous hands folded over the back of their necks and he shoved them toward the Asian man's booth.

"Where I come from it's an insult if you decline an invitation," the man said as they were shoved into the purple booth.

Adam and Lenny didn't answer. Instead, Adam straightened his jacket and discreetly pointed the hidden camera in his button directly onto the man's face. In the large circular booth, he looked even smaller than when he was standing. He had a light gray wool coat draped over his shoulders. Underneath that his black dress shirt looked like it might have been crafted from pure silk. He was well groomed and didn't look anything like the owner of a sleazy gentlemen's club. Not that Adam had the faintest idea what that would look like, but at first glance, he would've never guessed him to be involved in anything illegal.

"What are you doing in my club?" the man asked in perfect North American English.

"Oh, you're the owner! What a privilege to sit at your table, sir," Lenny blurted out.

What are you doing, Lenny?

Behind the owner's seemingly amused expression lay something far more dangerous.

"What are you doing in my club?" the club owner

asked again. This time his eyes held no hint of amusement.

"We'll go, sorry," Adam announced, attempting to get out of the booth.

But he barely got up from behind the table when a strong hand pushed him back down.

"You don't get to tell me when you're leaving. So I'm going to ask you both one more time, what are you doing in my club?"

Adam fell silent, praying Gabriel would now have enough reason to come barging through the doors and rescue them. But he didn't.

"I want my package back," Lenny suddenly spoke.

"Have you lost your mind?" Adam whispered sideways through pursed lips.

"Your friend seems to think you've lost your mind. I happen to agree."

"Agree, disagree, I don't care. I want what your big buffoon here stole from me the other day on the train."

The man let out a sadistic laugh.

"Is that so? I'm certain that little package of yours is worth far more to me than it is to you."

"That was my ticket out of here, man. Don't tell me it's worth more to you. You have no idea what it meant to me to finish that job. All you did was get me into a mess I now have no idea how to get out of!"

Lenny got the back of The Midget's hand across his face.

When he stopped seeing stars he spat a ball of bloodied saliva onto the table in front of him and turned to face the giant Black man.

"That's supposed to do what now, huh? Nothing my old man didn't do to me a thousand times as a kid." Lenny's eyes were fierce and unafraid.

His comment seemed to impress the kingpin. He sat there staring at them for what seemed like an eternity.

"I'll tell you what. Since you say this package is worth so much to you, how about I hire the two of you to do something for me? Get it right, and you're not only free to go, you can take your precious package back too."

"I'm listening," Lenny said.

What? Adam's mind responded as his heart skipped several beats.

The man pushed his chin out to one of his henchmen who disappeared behind the same red velvet curtain Lenny had said was concealing the poker den. Moments later he returned with Lenny's package in his hands.

"So you do have it?" Lenny immediately commented.

"I never said I didn't."

Adam and Lenny watched as the Asian man peeled back the seal and pulled a document from inside the envelope. He lay it in the center of the table.

"So, here's the deal. If you can figure out what this

document says, it's all yours and the two of you can leave."

Adam's eyes skimmed over the upside-down piece of paper. He recognized it immediately. It was a message written in a form of transposition cipher.

"Right, you're just gonna give it to me and let us walk out of here alive. Sure, man. I wasn't born yesterday," Lenny scoffed.

"I give you my word."

"Your word means nothing to me, man. I don't even know you. All I know is that you've already worked me over once. Who's to say you won't do it again?"

The man pushed his chin out again as he held out an open hand. A man behind his left shoulder handed him a wad of brand new hundred-dollar bills. He dropped it on the table in front of Lenny.

"Consider that my gesture of faith. I trust you to go find out what this document means and bring it back here. And you, in turn, trust me that I'll make good on my word upon your return. You have twenty-four hours."

Lenny shuffled uncomfortably. He had had his poker face on, playing the game with this thief, but now he had no idea how he'd give this man what he wanted.

"We'll do it," Adam suddenly interjected.

This time it was Lenny who cast a concerning eye his way.

"Good, we'll meet you back here tomorrow. Don't be late."

Lenny reached for the cash and the document and was quick to get up and get out of there. But Adam had stayed seated.

"We'll do you one better though. We don't need to come back tomorrow."

Lenny was certain he had a mini-stroke as he slumped back down into the booth.

"Oh, don't mind my friend here. We'll be back tomorrow evening. Let's go, Adam. This man has important business to tend to, and quite frankly, so do we." Lenny pushed against Adam's leg to prompt him to slide out of the booth.

"It's a type of cipher. I can tell you what it says in a couple of hours, but not here."

Lenny's face drained a pale white.

Adam had caught the attention of the club owner who sported a wide grin.

"Well, well, who would have thought. Looks like your little friend here has a few hidden talents no one knew about." He turned to Adam, his tone suddenly different, as if he was offended. "Why not here?"

Adam greatly wanted to avoid divulging that the real reason he wanted to get out of there was because, as a man of God, he felt extremely uncomfortable in the club —and that the time was fast approaching eight o'clock. So he offered him another excuse.

"I need silence and better lighting. Plus a writing pad and a pencil."

"Done," the Asian promptly agreed. He looked up at the giant.

"Jerome, put them in the penthouse and make sure they have what they need. And get them something to eat and drink too. Whatever they want."

The Midget gave a deep guttural growl under his breath.

"Yeah, yeah, calm down, tiger. It won't hurt you to be nice to our guests just this once. But I promise you this, if they don't deliver, I'll cut your chains and you can pull both of them apart one limb at a time. I'll let you pick which one you want to start with first."

CHAPTER EIGHTEEN

The penthouse was a magnificent suite on the top floor of a forty-story residential building in the most affluent part of the city. Overlooking the entire city from three sides, it took both Adam and Lenny's breath away the moment they stepped inside.

Lenny let out a long whistle of admiration as soon as the elevator doors opened and his eyes caught sight of the view.

"Now that's a view I can get used to," he poked fun at Jerome. "Who knows, you might soon be working for me."

The Midget wasn't amused. He had made that all too clear when he let out one of his now-iconic growls.

"Do you think you're a lion or some kind of beast or something that you need to growl every time someone tries to talk to you?" Lenny spoke his mind. "You know,

I don't want anyone with a negative attitude working for me. We might need to work on that before I hire you." Lenny knew he was pushing his luck, but he was also fully aware that Jerome wouldn't dare lift a finger to hurt them now that his boss needed their services. After all, he'd been told to make sure they were happy. But more than that, Lenny was desperate to rid his body and mind of the tension that seemed to have suddenly overwhelmed him.

Surprisingly, Jerome had enough self control—or sense—to turn around and leave, but not before he smashed his muscular body into Lenny's broken arm, seemingly accidental.

Lenny winced with pain.

"Oh, I'm definitely not hiring you now, man. You can forget about ever working for me!"

When the elevator doors closed behind Jerome and it was only Adam and Lenny left in the apartment, Lenny flopped down on one of the luxurious sofas and propped his feet up on top of the white marble coffee table.

"So our Asian host has money, and lots of it," Adam commented while scanning his hidden camera three hundred and sixty degrees through the suite.

"Keep your cover, boys," Gabriel announced in their ears. "I'm pretty sure he has a camera and mic on you."

Adam continued to walk through the spacious suite as if he needed to take it all in while Lenny made himself at home with a glass of expensive brandy from the drinks trolley.

"So here's what we know about our new friend," Gabriel continued. "His name is Quan Wu. Born and raised in Fujian, China where he studied biophysics. He then came to the US on a study visa and got his master's in biochemistry; graduated top of his class. He bounced back and forth between jobs in China and the US before finally buying out a large blue-chip pharmaceutical with a presence in Sweden, the UK, and here in the US. He's also linked to several small businesses across the US, hiding behind shell companies—no doubt for tax evasion or most likely money laundering. But no one's been able to tie him to any of these. My intel shows the man has power and he has connections and he's watching and listening to your every move as we speak. He's got hidden cameras all through the suite and audio listening in, but my team is working on obtaining the signal to block it."

Taking note of the information being fed through their earpieces, Adam swiftly took up his position at the large oval table—also crafted from white marble—that proudly stood in front of the main window. He organized the desk pad and the coded piece of writing in front of him and started working at cracking the message.

"Good, now pick up the phone and order the anchovy pizza with extra anchovies. My pizza delivery guy will plant a signal scrambler." Gabriel read out the phone number and Adam did as he was instructed.

Ten minutes later a young pizza guy delivered the food and promptly left. There was silence in their ears for another eight minutes or so while Lenny made himself comfortable with the pizza on the white leather sofa, and Adam continued with the code.

Then suddenly Gabriel spoke again.

"Got it! We're in and all signals have successfully been blocked. It won't take them too long to figure out what's happening but you can speak freely now, boys."

"Well, that took you long enough, Major. The clock is ticking, man. I have to get this package to Diaz before he kills my sister. How am I supposed to do that when Preacher here got us trapped in this palace?" Lenny expressed his pent-up frustration.

"There was no way I could have known Wu was going to lock us up in his glass tower, Lenny. I'm sorry. I was only trying to save us time. If we had agreed to his twenty-four-hour timeline we wouldn't have had enough time to meet Diaz—Carrie would have stood no chance. At least now we have time to give Wu what he wants *and*, may I remind you, we walk out of here alive, in time to get the package to Diaz. Not to even mention the added bonus of all that 'good faith' money you stuck in your pocket."

Lenny was anxiously pacing the room, his good hand behind his neck.

"I can't believe I've actually got the package in hand and no way of getting it to Diaz to save my sister. It's not as if the man will accept a fax, you know," he huffed, visibly distraught about the situation. "And I don't even know how we're going to talk our way out of giving Wu what he wants. How are we supposed to know what a bunch of scrambled letters on that stupid piece of paper means? This has just gone from bad to worse." Lenny was beside himself.

"I'm going to let you handle this, Adam," Gabriel said, his voice laced with amusement.

Adam picked up the piece of paper and walked over to where Lenny was now about to pour himself another drink.

"You don't need another drink, Lenny. We've got this."

"Really? And you figure this how, exactly? We're kind of in a pickle here, Preacher," he said, lifting the glass to his mouth.

Adam took the drink from Lenny's hand and placed it back on the bar trolley.

"Like I said, we've got this. I've already cracked the message."

The look on Lenny's face was one of pure incredulity.

"You didn't. You've *already* unscrambled those letters? When? How?"

"Just now, while you threw your little hissy fit and

got all up in my face. I knew what this was the second I saw it. My father used to give me these to do all the time. Of course, I didn't even realize what he was teaching me back then. I thought it was just a fun activity, like crossword puzzles."

Lenny grabbed the paper from Adam's hand and scanned through it.

"This isn't a crossword puzzle. There aren't any clues."

"No, it's not. It's a rail fence cipher. One of the most commonly used transposition ciphers during World War Two. And a really simple one too. See these lines? Now imagine they are rails running diagonally. The plain text is written downwards and then diagonally on these rails. The message is read like a zigzag—down and up moving across the three rails."

Lenny stared at the writing.

"Nope, still don't get it. Looks like Greek to me."

"Well, that's because they combined it with a route cipher, obviously to make the encryption a bit harder to read at first glance. See the route cipher is a block instead of the rails, and the text is read in a diagonal wave, not a zigzag. But you're right, these were actually designed by the ancient Greeks."

Lenny still had a blank look on his face.

"Okay, clearly you're the genius, Preacher, and that's fine. It doesn't need to make sense to me. I just need to get this to Diaz so I can save my sister's life."

Adam smiled. "I want that too, Lenny. But something tells me this decryption is just the beginning of our relationship with Wu. Once he reads this message he's not going to let us go."

He had Lenny intrigued and Gabriel quickly prompted Adam to go ahead and share the information.

"Fellows, I believe we have found ourselves smack bang in the middle of a corporate espionage deal. In fact, I think I've figured out what all the tail clues are."

"Great work, Adam, but we're going to have to pause on that for now. They're outside the building. Seems our scramblers have finally flagged them that something's up."

"What about Carrie? I need to get this to Diaz. We're running out of time," Lenny expressed his frustration.

"Adam, can you stall them with a red herring?" Gabriel asked.

"Copy that. But just so you're aware, the decoded message is in fact instructions to collect another package. It won't take him long to discover we duped him."

"Time's up," Gabriel warned moments before the elevator doors opened and Wu and two of his sidekicks entered.

Lenny was back on the couch eating more pizza, and Adam pretended to still be at it with the coded message.

Wu wasn't very big in stature but he had quite the presence when he walked into the room—as was often the case when arrogance and pride ruled in man's heart.

But arrogance ruled in Lenny's heart too and he seemed unperturbed by Wu's arrival. He already knew they had what he needed.

Wu ignored Lenny where he lay on the sofa and approached Adam at the table. He leaned in over his left shoulder without uttering a single word.

In one swift unsuspecting motion, Wu had Adam in a chokehold and pinned his face down onto the white marble table.

CHAPTER NINETEEN

Adam didn't fight Wu's grip. He was outnumbered in any event. Instead, his mind wandered to one of his favorite psalms. *Keep me as the apple of your eye; hide me in the shadow of your wings.* And as he prayed that Wu didn't discover the device in his ear or the hidden microphone on his chest, he prayed for God to give him the wisdom to say the right thing.

"I am nobody's fool," Wu's stern voice spoke next to his ear. "If I find out you lied to me you won't live to tell anyone about it."

"I didn't lie. I can decode the text."

Wu tightened his arm around Adam's throat. To the point where Adam thought he was going to stop breathing altogether.

"Leave him alone!" Lenny yelled from where The Midget was holding him down on the sofa.

"Why? He's a liar and I don't like being lied to."

"He's not a liar. He's telling the truth."

Wu released his grip around Adam's neck. He pushed his face down onto the paper as a final gesture of his power. And as he stepped back and got busy straightening his red silk jacket, he signaled for Jerome to let go of Lenny too.

Wu stood in front of the large window and took in the view, arms folded behind his back. In a gentler tone, a complete contrast to the aggressive man who'd existed mere moments ago, he asked if they had managed to get their coffee.

The question caught both Adam and Lenny off guard. So when Wu turned around to face them, neither was able to hide their shocked expressions. It was Adam who answered.

"Actually, we got a pizza instead."

Wu's eyes narrowed. His lips curled into the faintest of smiles. As if he knew something, suspected what was going on.

But Adam somehow contained the fear that threatened to lodge in his throat. Lenny, for once, was speechless. His tongue held captive by God's divine power.

"Good, we wouldn't want you to get coffee instead of food, now would we?"

He knows!

Wu turned to face Lenny.

"So Lucky Lenny here says you can decrypt the text."

Lenny's eyes instantly filled with surprise which was precisely the pleasurable reaction Wu had hoped to get from his words.

"Oh now, come on. You didn't think I'd let two strangers into my property without finding out exactly who I'm in business with, did you? The question is, do you know who you are dealing with?"

Unlike Lenny who was visibly too afraid to answer, Adam recognized it was just Wu's pitiful tactic to scare them.

"I think we do, but it's irrelevant at this point. And yes, I did decrypt the text. The decoded message is written out here on the legal pad. I gave you what you wanted and therefore we are no longer in business," Adam said bravely without a quiver in his voice.

This time it was Wu who was surprised.

"Did you now?"

"Uh-huh, and since we can see you're a man of your word, Lenny and I will now let you get on with your business."

Adam pushed himself away from the table and reached for the envelope containing the original message. As he turned to leave, Lenny in tow, Wu's voice stopped them.

"Not so fast, Adam Cross."

Addressing Adam by name was yet another attempt to flaunt his power.

Wu continued. "You see, while I am a man of my word, I believe I also told you not to take me for a fool. Our little agreement didn't involve any, shall we say, *third* party. So you see, now I find myself in a rather precarious position. If I let the two of you walk out of this building, I'll be opening myself up to having to entertain a new set of visitors. And truth be told I'm not that fond of these visitors. Frankly, I don't enjoy coffee."

Adam and Lenny were silent for what seemed like hours before Adam finally spoke. "We don't like coffee either. In fact, as a gesture of faith, we'll walk out of here with you. I give you my word that you won't be receiving any unwanted guests. Our business isn't with you. All we want is the package so Lenny here can complete the job he was hired to do. That's it. And by the time he delivers the envelope, and they've managed to decipher the code, you'll have completed your transaction and the deal will be done. It's a win-win for all."

Wu's small eyes were locked and focused on Adam's face as if he was trying to detect if Adam was tricking him. Neither spoke nor moved a muscle. It was a staredown that left Lenny's insides tense with fear, and Adam clinging to God in faith.

Behind him, Jerome growled again.

"Now, now, Jerome, today may not have been the

day you got your little treat as promised, but I think Lenny can attest firsthand how quickly you can track him down."

"So we have an agreement?" Adam said, eager to get out of there.

"For now, but Adam, if you betray my trust, you won't live to see another day."

ADAM AND LENNY MADE IT BACK TO THEIR MOTEL IN one piece. Tanisha and Gabriel were both in their room when they burst through the door.

"That was intense, man. I for sure thought that giant was going to rip me apart today," Lenny said as he flopped down onto his bed. "I mean, did you see that guy's hands? He'd break my bones like they were toothpicks."

Adam handed Gabriel the envelope.

"Now what? It won't take long for Wu to figure out that I sent him on a wild goose chase." He glanced at his watch. "And the clock's ticking. We need to get the package to Diaz."

Gabriel studied the cipher.

"You said you've figured out the tail clues?" he asked.

Adam took a seat at the table and spread open the newspaper codes.

"I think so, yes. We already know these are all locations where transactions took place. More importantly, I think I've figured out that they're selling inside information—corporate intel, trade secrets, that type of thing. I would assume this Diaz guy is the matchmaker, the go-between. The guy who brings the buyers and sellers together. Wu is a buyer who intercepted a deal. People like him want to cut out the middleman. Now, the addresses are obvious, but the tails of these clues are what determine the product. So we have *shoes*, that's corporate espionage, like in this case someone like Nike. *MC two* is in fact mc squared. That's calling for pharmaceuticals or biotech firms—they're selling a secret formula. *Triple Long* I believe is a Wall Street term traders use to describe a blue-chip company, so that's stocks or Bitcoin et cetera. That's how they match the right buyers to whatever it is that's up for sale. It's literally an advert. My guess is that whichever buyer is interested at the time, contacts them back somehow. Perhaps there's even an auction of some kind."

Gabriel grinned with admiration.

"Your father would be so proud of you right now, Adam. Great job my friend. Your theory certainly fits Wu's profile, which means at the end of this rainbow there should be a formula of some kind, and whoever Lenny was meant to deliver this envelope to, is the original buyer. Now that we know what they're all up to and what to look for, I'm going to hand it off to Corporate

Crimes and let them bring these guys down. Our job is to get Carrie back before both Diaz and Wu catch on." Gabriel turned to Lenny. "Make contact with Diaz and arrange the trade, Lenny. We'll have eyes and ears on you at all times."

AN HOUR LATER LENNY HEADED TOWARD THE PLACE under the bridge where he knew Diaz usually met up with the courier runners. He was nervous. Even more than the previous time when he went back begging for a job. A decision he now deeply regretted. As he walked the half block from the train station, he sent a message to the universe to tell Carrie he was on his way. When he had finished repeating it in his head, it suddenly occurred to him that perhaps this was what praying was. Perhaps he'd been talking to God all this time and just never knew it. The thought made him smile and he liked the way it made him feel.

When the bridge came into view, his body stiffened and he felt a familiar flutter in the pit of his stomach.

"Can you guys hear me?" he spoke quietly.

"Loud and clear, Lenny. We got eyes on you too. Remember, just act normal. Set up the place to do the trade and then walk away."

Lenny confirmed it.

As he rounded the corner he saw Diaz in his spot

under the bridge talking with what Lenny assumed must have been another courier. His heart pounded hard against his chest. His palms felt clammy.

Diaz suddenly spotted him and quickly sent the runner on his way. His eyes met with Lenny's. *Keep it together, Leonard. You can do this.* He stopped a few feet away from Diaz, wearing his best poker face.

"I'm going to assume the reason you're here is to let me know that you have my package," Diaz said.

"Yes. Where's my sister?"

"Where's my package?"

"Not before I see Carrie."

"You're lying."

"I'm not. I have it."

"You're a poker player, Lenny. But don't underestimate me. I know a bluff when I see one."

Lenny pulled his phone from his pocket. His thumb rolled over the screen until he found the photo. Gabriel had taken a photo of the envelope lying next to that day's newspaper. He held it out for Diaz to see, pointing out the timestamp.

"I have the package. You'll get it when I get my sister back. Meet me back here at ten p.m. With my sister of course. And, Diaz, you had better not have hurt one single hair on her head."

Lenny turned and walked away. He dared not look back. His heart was pounding so hard and fast he thought he was going to be sick. He had done it. In a couple of hours, he would see his little sister again, for the first time in years. And when he got her home to her husband and daughter again, he'd go out and get a real job and pay back every dime he owed to everyone he was indebted to.

CHAPTER TWENTY

The night didn't quite feel as cold when Lenny walked the now familiar footpath through the park to where it ran underneath the arched train bridge. Perhaps it was because his veins were surging with adrenaline. Or perhaps it was because he'd see Carrie again. He wasn't sure. Either way, he had a hard time breathing normally—or at all.

As he struggled to calm his racing heart, he was surprised by how much he suddenly yearned to have a normal life, a fresh start. And how badly he wanted to get the deal done so he'd have a chance of turning his life around. One that was free from all things illegal. One that included his sister. And one in which he didn't feel so alone.

It was a full moon and Lenny could see almost all

the way down the path to where Diaz and he were to meet under the bridge. He wasn't there yet.

He checked the time on his mobile phone. He was ten minutes early. He looked back to where Gabriel had said his men would be on standby—should anything go wrong.

The small tactical team was nearby—hidden in a van disguised as a plumber's vehicle. Adam had stayed at the motel with Gabriel.

Now at the meeting point under the bridge, an owl hooted from a nearby tree. It made the atmosphere even more eerie. In hindsight, he should have chosen a more public place.

He decided to stick to the areas where the moonlight hit the most—so Gabriel's men could see him better.

Glancing at the time again it was one minute before ten. There was still neither sight nor sound of Diaz. His forefinger and thumb tightened on the yellow envelope. What if Diaz didn't show? What if Carrie was already dead? What if he'd been bluffing and she was already safely home? They hadn't even bothered to check. The thoughts suddenly left him even more restless. He contemplated whispering into his mic to ask Gabriel to check, but if Diaz was nearby it would blow his cover. All he could do now was wait.

Another two minutes passed and Diaz was nowhere to be seen. Lenny wasn't anxious anymore. He was starting to get angry, frustrated. The owl above his head suddenly went quiet. There was a shuffle of approaching feet coming from the other end. He peered into the dark shadows under the bridge. Listened. His entire body was sweaty and rigid.

In his ear, a male voice told him he had eyes on the target. Lenny strained his eyes. He couldn't see anyone yet. The shuffling grew louder and Lenny's heart skipped several beats. Almost instantly Diaz's pointy black shoes and the bottom half of his jeans became visible in the soft moonlight. Soon after, the outlines of his tall body under his long black coat came into view. Lenny's fingers clamped down on the envelope. He was ready. Then he saw his face; Diaz was looking at him from under a bright beam of moonlight. His expression was off, cold, almost cautionary. Lenny tore his eyes away from his face and searched for his sister behind him. He heard more than one set of footsteps. She had to be there too. Diaz stopped three yards away from him, his face stern. His eyes pulled into a squint. Demanding Lenny look at him.

In the hollow echoes of the space under the bridge, Lenny heard faint whimpering. *Carrie!* Every cell in his body was on full alert. He held back his raging emotions. Neither of them spoke. They just stood there, staring, waiting to see who'd draw their metaphorical gun first.

It was Diaz who caved. His eyes dropped to the yellow envelope in Lenny's hand. Then suddenly his eyes searched the distance behind him. He seemed on edge. *Something's wrong.* Lenny's gut warned him to be careful. To get the deal done and get out of there.

"Where's my sister?"

Silence. Then Diaz finally spoke.

"Why do you keep doing this, Lenny?"

His question had Lenny draw his eyebrows into a frown.

"What?"

"Why can't you ever just stick to one deal, huh, Lenny? Why do you always have to play both sides? Be greedy."

Lenny's pounding heart dropped into his stomach.

"I don't know what you mean. Where's my sister?"

"Did you really think I wasn't going to find out, huh? You must think I'm an idiot."

"Look, Diaz, I don't know what you're on about, man. I have your package. I just want my sister back so let's get this over with."

Diaz clicked his tongue behind his teeth.

"Our deal is off."

"What? No! You can't change our deal. Carrie! Carrie!"

She didn't answer.

"Oh, but I can, *Lucky Lenny*." He emphasized his name sarcastically. "You see, that piece of paper is now worthless. It's hot; too risky since you tried to pull a side hustle with Dr. Wu. None of my clients want to come near it now. You just couldn't help yourself now could you, Lenny?"

"You're wrong. I didn't make any deals with him."

"Stop taking me for an idiot! You helped him. That spells treachery to me. Betrayal in its finest form."

"How else was I supposed to get it back? He stole it from me in the first place. I did what I had to do."

"Well look where that's gotten you. Word got out and now my real buyer's out a commodity. And I'm out of my commission. Do you have any idea how long I've been working on this deal? Two years, Lenny! And no one's been able to get it done."

Lenny's mind went to the girl at the newsstand whose boyfriend had perished at the hand of Diaz and this deal.

"That's not my problem, Diaz. I did my part. I got you your package back. We had a deal! Carrie!" he called out to her.

"Not your problem, huh? Well, we'll see about that!"

Lenny watched in horror as Diaz raised one arm to signal someone in the shadows behind him.

The loud clap of a single gunshot resounded through the hollow darkness.

Lenny heard a body drop to the ground.

Saw the satisfaction in Diaz's eyes.

"No! Carrie! Carrie!"

He stormed toward the dark space.

Moments later he felt the hard knock against his skull.

And everything went quiet around him.

ADAM PACED THE SMALL MOTEL ROOM AS HE LISTENED to the transmission. The gunshot blasted loudly in his ear. His heart went cold. His legs threatened to give way.

"Tell me that didn't just happen!" he yelled out to Gabriel who was already in communication with his tactical team.

"Gabriel! Are they alive?"

Please, Father, let them be alive!

Gabriel didn't answer immediately.

"Talk to me, Gabriel. What's going on?" he tried again.

This time Gabriel answered, the satphone still squeezed against his ear.

"We're not sure yet, tactical's making their way to the scene."

Adam paced again, his heavy heart and mind now fully tuned to God to intervene.

"Lenny, can you hear me?" Gabriel called through the transmission to Lenny's earpiece.

He didn't answer.

"How did this happen, Gabriel? Your team was right

there," Adam said, his voice strained in an effort not to sound accusing.

"I'm sorry, Adam. Diaz took us by surprise. We should have some answers very soon."

Gabriel's words had barely been spoken when his attention was drawn back to the voice in the receiver.

When he ended the call with the leader of his tactical team he paused as if to find the right words before he spoke.

"Lenny's okay, he's alive. They just knocked him unconscious, but he'll be fine. Two of my men are on their way here with him."

"And Carrie? What about Carrie?"

"No sign of her."

"But we heard them shoot her?"

"No, we heard a gunshot and assumed they shot her. We don't know that they shot her for certain."

"So there's no dead body or any trace of her?"

"They did find blood, not Lenny's. They're waiting for CSI to take a sample to analyze. I'm told their mobile unit's equipment is sophisticated enough to determine if it is human and if so, whether it's male or female. Getting an identity will take time but they'll put a rush on it for us. But until we know for certain we need to assume she's still alive."

Adam slumped down in a nearby chair.

"Okay, now what? If we're to assume he never brought her there in the first place, and that she's still alive, how do we find her? We don't have any bargaining chips left. The deal's dead in the water," Adam reasoned.

"Not necessarily," Tanisha announced. She had been quietly listening in the background.

Her comment caught both men off guard.

"We're listening," Gabriel said.

"We can create a new buyer. Bring the deal back to life. Diaz said his current buyers are no longer interested. But if there was a new buyer…"

"He'd need the package again," Adam said.

"Exactly. All we have to do is find out how the buyers communicate with them," Tanisha continued.

"I like it," Gabriel announced. "But time isn't our friend; now more than ever. If Diaz doesn't have use for Carrie anymore, he'll get rid of her."

"Agreed. We've got our work cut out for us but at least we have a plan."

Just then a knock at the door announced Lenny's arrival.

"Great to see you're alive, Lenny," Adam welcomed him back cheerfully which invited a scornful look from Lenny.

"I wish I wasn't," he said. "And why are you so chipper, huh? Or was all that 'Carrie and everyone in Turtle Cove mean so much to me' blabber all fake? They killed her, man. They killed her right in front of me." Lenny broke down and sobbed.

"We don't know that Lenny," Adam spoke gently.

"I was there, remember? She was there! I heard her."

"But did you actually see her, physically?" Gabriel asked.

"No, but I heard their feet shuffling, and her body fall to the ground when they shot her," he said sobbing again.

"Lenny, you need to stay positive. There's no evidence that it was her. You didn't see her. It could have been anyone. Diaz went there knowing the deal was dead. He didn't intend doing any trading with you. It's fair to say he was bluffing, intentionally wanting to torture you."

Gabriel's satphone bleeped.

"Thank you, lieutenant. Appreciate the urgency."

The expectant look on Adam's face had Lenny suddenly worried.

"What? Who was that?"

"That was CSI. They've done an analysis of the blood found at the scene. It was human."

Lenny sobbed again.

Adam fell silent, waiting for Gabriel to speak the words he'd been praying not to hear.

"It was female."

CHAPTER TWENTY-ONE

For the next few minutes, the room was quiet. No one spoke. Lenny had taken to his bed and sat there clutching his knees to his chest, convinced his sister had been killed. Guilt for dragging her into his world was tearing him apart. He was an emotional mess and he let everyone in the room know it.

"I'll whip up some of my famous fried chicken and corn grits," Tanisha announced, then quickly slipped out the door. She wasn't one to easily show emotion, they all knew that. But it was clear she had no idea how to handle the situation.

"Sounds good, thanks, Tanisha," Adam said then went and took a seat on the foot of Lenny's bed.

"Lenny, we should wait until the forensic test results come back. Let's not assume that it was Carrie. We need to stay strong now and try to revive this deal while there's still time."

"How do you do it, huh, Preacher? You lost your wife and daughter to a maniac. Your entire life got ruined. How do you still sit there all positive and stuff?"

"How can I not? Losing them was the worst thing that's ever happened to me, but afterward, after I grieved, I knew I had to make a choice. I could let the man who did that to them also consume and destroy my life, or I could choose to see all the good I still have in my life and trust that God will redirect his plan for me. I chose the latter."

"Well, newsflash. There's no good left in my life. I have no family, no real friends, I'm up to my eyeballs in debt with some seriously dangerous people, I have nothing. My life is an empty chasm. And as for your God, he doesn't want anything to do with a lowlife scumbag like me."

"Yeah, well, you see, that's where you're wrong, my friend. If not for Carrie's kidnapping, we would've never become friends, and Gabriel here would've not had any new leads to hunt and take down one of the biggest crime syndicates this country has ever seen. Something the authorities have been working on for years. And… you would never have seen the opportunity God's giving you now. All through the Bible, God chose people just like you to do his work for him. Even the disciples he chose were lowly fishermen from Galilee—a place that was considered to be on the wrong side of the tracks. He also chose Matthew, a tax collector who made it his profession to extort the needy. God isn't picky, Lenny. So, how about we put our trust in his plan for your life and allow God to help us get Carrie back?"

"You really think she's still alive?"

"I do."

"Fine, then I'll take your word for it since you and God are so close an' all."

"I'm only telling you what has been my experience, Lenny. If you look at your life carefully, you'll see God working. And when you are ready, I'll introduce you to him so you can experience his grace firsthand. But for now, we need to get Carrie back."

"I'd love that, Preacher, but Diaz made it very clear he wants nothing to do with this package. And without the package we—"

Adam interrupted him.

"We have a plan. Actually, Tanisha came up with it. We're going to create a new buyer, bring the deal back to life. And Diaz will have no choice but to come crawling back to you for the package. That's how we'll get Carrie back."

Just then Tanisha entered with a trolley full of her famous southern cooking. She left it just inside the door and hurried over to where Gabriel still sat at the table.

Anxious to get something off her chest, she dropped two piles of newspapers on Adam's bed.

"Something struck me as very odd while I was cooking, the dates on the newspapers. Look."

She spread out about a dozen newspapers on the bed.

"Take a look at these over here. These are the copies in which you found the other ciphers. See the print dates? They're spaced out. Evenly spaced out."

"Precisely two days apart," Adam commented.

"Yes exactly. Now this pile over here is from the dates in between those days. They didn't have the same ciphers in them."

"But those might be the papers in which the buyers answered them with a different cipher," Adam finished her thought.

"That's what I was thinking, yes. We just need to look for it," Tanisha said as she strolled over to the food trolley and started dishing up plates for everyone.

"Great job, Tanisha," Gabriel said. "Shall we split these up between us? Adam, any idea what we might be looking for?"

He was already busy with one of the papers.

"Look for anything out of the ordinary first. An upside-down ad, a missing word, anything that looks out of place."

Adam looked at his wristwatch.

"Yeah, I know, I'm already on it," Gabriel announced.

"What? Am I missing something again?" Lenny asked feeling slightly lost in the events.

"If we find a cipher, we'd have to find a way of getting it printed in tomorrow's newspaper. It's just gone midnight. The paper will be out in three hours," Adam explained while scanning through the prints.

"Oh, we can't wait another day, Adam. If there's a chance my sister is still alive there's no telling what Diaz might do to her now that he doesn't need her. What are we going to do?" Lenny's voice escalated into a panic.

"Already taken care of," Gabriel said as he ended a call. "I just got off the phone with the editor in chief. We have two hours before they go to print."

"And we can trust him?" Tanisha queried.

"We have no choice but to. But I guess if word gets out then we know that Diaz has him in his pocket."

THE SMALL TEAM CONTINUED SCANNING THROUGH EACH of the papers. Forty minutes later, it was Lenny who spoke first.

"I might be seeing double but I've been around enough crossword puzzles to know this doesn't look right. I have my mother to thank for that."

He pointed at the row of letters that was printed upside down just below the daily crossword puzzle.

"See, usually they print the answers upside down, but this is just a jumble of letters. Not even the spaces in between the letters are even."

Adam leaned in over Lenny's shoulder then hurriedly opened his paper to the same page.

"I have one too," he announced

"Me too," Tanisha announced.

"So that's another cipher. I don't recognize it though," Gabriel said.

"Why are you searching through the for-sale papers?" Lenny questioned Adam when he suddenly started opening the cipher pile's newspapers.

"If they're in these papers too then we might be wrong. But if they're not—"

"Then we've found our communication trail," Gabriel finished.

It didn't take them long to establish that the cipher pile's papers didn't have the jumbled upside-down sentences beneath their crossword puzzles.

"Well, Lenny, it seems you have an eye for detail. Well spotted, buddy," Adam said as he started transferring the letter sequences to his legal pad.

"Any idea what we're looking at? We're shaving it a bit thin. We have less than an hour to get this to the editor," Gabriel announced from where he was working through the ciphers alongside Adam.

"Not yet, but I don't believe it's a transposition cipher, plus there are numbers added into the mix."

"Agreed. Doesn't look like a substitution either."

"Perhaps some sort of a lexicon cipher, or a combination of more than one?"

Adam and Gabriel went back and forth trying to crack the code. Silence prevailed for several more minutes.

"Uh, I don't want to add pressure but we're running out of time." Lenny spoke from across the room.

He got no response from either of them.

A moment later Gabriel and Adam spoke simultaneously.

"It's a scytale cipher!"

The moments that followed were a mad flurry as the men worked their way through the newspapers. Then they rummaged through every drawer and cupboard before they finally regrouped around the table. Yes, their adrenaline was pumping because they were running out of time, but more than that, they looked like two excited kids on Christmas morning.

Lenny and Tanisha watched as they tore the letter sequences from the newspapers and wrapped them around every cylindrical object they could find.

"Nope, too thin," Adam announced.

"This one doesn't work either," Gabriel answered.

"Got it!" Adam announced when he had neatly

coiled the ribbon of paper around a drinking straw from one of their soda cans.

"Okay, I can't hold it back any longer," Lenny exclaimed. "What the heck are you guys doing?"

"It's a scytale code," Adam answered briefly, deep in concentration while he wrote down the first three messages.

"You said that yes. Still means nothing."

"It's another ancient Greek code. Back then the cipher text was written on parchment and wound around a baton. Without the cylinder, it's just oddly spaced letters. But when you coil it around an object similar in dimensions, the letters line up to spell out the message."

"There's a pattern here, Adam. This is definitely how the buyers make their requests known. Look, this is the one Wu intercepted. *Seek MC two. Hot ten.* Diaz then answered the following day with the address and time to meet."

He glanced at the time.

"We have ten minutes."

Adam ripped a piece of paper from his legal pad, coiled it around the drinking straw, and configured the cipher. He used the identical code sequence then handed it to Gabriel to send off to the editor.

"Now what?" Lenny said when it was done.

"Now we get some rest and wait until Diaz gets the morning paper. If we're right, and this fishing expedition of ours works, then you'll be getting a call from Diaz before the sun is up," Adam predicted.

"And the buyer?" Lenny asked, looking concerned.

"There is no buyer. We'll have handed him the package in exchange for Carrie by the time he figures out there was no buyer to begin with. We'll be a solid twenty-four hours ahead of him," Adam explained.

"And since we'd have Carrie back safely, and you'd all be out of harm's way, it makes for the perfect time to catch the guy redhanded and blow this entire syndicate out of the water. The moment we have your sister back, I'll have the Corporate Crimes unit move in. Diaz will have someone to meet him the day after tomorrow, it just won't be who he'll be expecting," Gabriel added with a twisted smile.

"And if our editor is dirty?" Tanisha interjected.

Gabriel didn't have to answer her. His eyes said it all. If Diaz had the editor in chief of one of the biggest newspapers in the country in his pocket, their plan would be foiled.

And Carrie would be dead—if she were in fact still alive.

CHAPTER TWENTY-TWO

It was in the early hours of the morning, just as the sun started rising, that the piercing sound of Lenny's mobile phone echoed through the small room. Since they'd only got to bed a few hours earlier, neither Adam nor Lenny woke up the first time the phone signaled an incoming call. It was only when the phone rang for the second time, that Lenny reached for it, nearly knocking it off the side table in his sleepy state.

"Yes?" he said still half asleep, his voice groggy.

"It seems Lady Luck has dealt you a good hand today, Lenny."

Lenny wiped his hand over his face in an attempt to wake up. The sudden realization of whose voice it was, had him alert and fully awake in a second.

"Diaz?"

But the voice that replied wasn't that of Diaz. It was

a female. One whose voice Lenny didn't recognize at first.

"Leonard, it's me, Carrie."

The voice jerked Lenny to an upright position.

"Carrie? Is that you? You're alive! Are you okay?" he rambled.

She didn't answer. Instead, Diaz spoke again.

"If you want to see her again bring the package. And this time, Lenny, come alone or they will find her corpse next to yours."

Diaz ended the call.

"Hello? Carrie, Diaz…" But the line was dead.

"You spoke to Carrie?" asked Adam, who was now also awake and sitting up in bed.

"Briefly, yes. She's alive, Adam! She's alive."

"I am extremely relieved to hear that. So what time and where?"

"He didn't say. I'm assuming it's the usual spot under the bridge. He did say though to come alone this time."

"So he knew he was being watched."

"Yep, that's possibly why he never properly came out of the shadows."

"Or he watched from somewhere after he had left and saw the tactical unit arrive at the scene."

Lenny was out of bed and already making his way to the bathroom.

"Either way, I can't risk it. I have to go there on my own this time."

"That's too dangerous, Lenny. I'm sure Gabriel can instruct his team to be a bit more discreet this time round."

"No, Adam! I'm not going to take any chances with this man. He said to come alone or he'll kill us both. And as we have all seen he is quite capable of doing that. He would have no reason to kill us once he has the package. It's just another transaction for him. But the very instant he sees the authorities, he'll back out again."

Adam scooped several spoons of ground coffee in the drip filter machine and flipped on the switch.

"I hate to say this, Lenny but you're right. It's too risky. We're not there to catch him. We're there to make sure Carrie comes home safely."

As expected, Gabriel wasn't in favor of Lenny going to meet Diaz on his own. But once he too realized that Carrie was Diaz's only bargaining tool, he conceded. And since he was meeting him in broad daylight, it decreased further the element of risk. He did however make Lenny wear a bulletproof vest and a hidden camera and mic.

Once again Lenny took the pedestrian path down

towards the bridge where Diaz would have his usual meetings at a set time with his runners. It was noon. As he neared the spot, he saw that Diaz wasn't in his usual position. He checked the time on his watch. Pondered if perhaps the schedule had since changed. He'd wait a little longer. He turned around to inspect the area, but there was no sign of Diaz. In his earpiece Gabriel prompted for information but deciding it was too risky to speak in the event Diaz was watching him, Lenny made a guttural sound to indicate the opposite without moving his lips.

"Copy that," Gabriel said. "Wait it out a bit longer. Chances are he's scouting the surrounds to see if you've come alone."

But twenty minutes later Diaz was still nowhere to be found. Holding his cover Lenny didn't do anything to suggest that he wasn't alone, but frustration and disappointment overwhelmed him. When another ten minutes had passed he decided to abort the mission and started making his way back up the path. And as his mind raced with prospective reasons as to why Diaz hadn't turned up, he found himself asking God how all of this could be part of some divine plan. The thought caught him off guard since he'd never prayed before—or recognized God. Could Adam be right? Was the misery in his life all part of some greater scheme? Then if so, what was God waiting for?

He brushed the thought away as he neared the end of the footpath. All he could think about now was that their own plan had failed. Perhaps Tanisha's gut instinct was right in that the editor was dirty. Perhaps Diaz had realized it was a trap.

As he approached the busy road he needed to cross to walk the few blocks back to where Adam was waiting for him in his car, he slipped the envelope inside his jacket and half under his armpit. From the corner of his eye, he spotted a white vehicle driving too close to the sidewalk where he needed to cross. Drawing closer he noticed it was slowing down. At first, he thought it was the tactical team since the van appeared to look the same. But when it was just a few yards away, he instantly recognized the driver. By then, it was already too late.

It took all of three short seconds for the van to pull up beside him and for two strong men to yank him into the back of the minivan.

"No, please! Let me go! Let me out, please!" he begged as he wrestled his captors.

But the men had no mercy on him and with one fell swoop of a right hook against his left eye, Lenny collapsed into the van.

While Adam sat helpless in his car listening to the horrifying ordeal play out mere blocks away, he found his soul suddenly in turmoil. It took all he had to cling on to his faith, to believe that God was still in control. He yanked his earpiece from his ear and disconnected the mic—desperate to have a private moment with God. When he knew he had broken the transmission, he recited several scriptures out loud, spoke God's word over the situation, and prayed that His will would prevail. And as he did that his heart slowly filled with peace. Peace that it would all turn out exactly as God intended it. Because, although he could find no humanly justifiable reason why Lenny, once again, had fallen victim to a senseless situation, he knew without a doubt that another power was also at work. For he had seen this kind of spiritual warfare before when the enemy worked hard to keep a soul from yielding his life to God. The thought set him at ease. If the enemy was working that hard to keep Lenny's soul captive, it meant Lenny's heart was busy changing. And God was at work.

As he prepared to turn his car around to head back to the motel, an oncoming vehicle came into view in his rearview mirror. With his eyes on it, waiting for it to pass so he could turn around, he recognized the driver. That was no coincidence, he thought.

The white van wheeled past him and something stirred inside him. As if an invisible force took over the car's wheel he suddenly found himself following the van. With his hands clasped tightly over the steering wheel, his body taut and hunched forward in his seat, he kept his sights pinned on the vehicle. Careful not to be detected, he held back just enough to stay on its tail.

"Gabriel," he called out, forgetting he had removed his earpiece. He looked down to find it, just briefly, but when he looked up again, the van was gone.

"No, no, no!" he yelled out in annoyance. *Help me find it, Lord.*

He increased speed while his eyes frantically searched for the white panel van. He rounded the corner, looked back just in case he missed it, and pushed his car down the side street. For a split second, he thought he shouldn't have taken the turn. He pulled over to the left and checked his mirrors for oncoming cars—so he could turn back. The road was too busy. So he continued on to the next junction. As he prepared to make a u-turn he spotted the van parked at the corner on the opposite side of the road. So focused was he on the van that he didn't see the oncoming car. As the approaching car's horn blasted him to attention, he swerved to avoid it and narrowly missed two more.

When he finally managed to safely park in a nearby parking space, his heart was beating a hundred miles an hour. With the front of his car now pointed in the direction of the van, he took a few moments to catch his breath. He peered up at the tall buildings on either side of the parked van. They had to be in one of them. His fingers fumbled to find his earpiece. When he reconnected his transmission radio he made contact with Gabriel.

"Why did you break comms, Adam? I was worried sick," Gabriel said.

"Sorry, I just needed a private moment. More importantly, I think I might have found Lenny. I'm not positive but I think I'm right."

"It's our only shot so I'll take it. We lost his comms and tracker the moment they took him. Give me your location and I'll send a team. And, Adam, do not leave your car, understood? Just wait there for my men to arrive."

"Copy that."

Adam shared his location and made it clear to Gabriel to tell his tactical team to come unannounced. Any wrong moves now and both Lenny and Carrie could end up dead.

If it had been anyone else that had taken Lenny he would have been a lot more at ease. But considering how their last meeting had ended, and how they had intentionally deceived him, Wu had every reason to settle the score.

CHAPTER TWENTY-THREE

Lenny found himself in a small, deserted warehouse. When he couldn't move he discovered that his feet were tethered to the legs of a steel chair. Similarly, his arms were pulled back around the backrest and bound by cable ties. Where they had punched him, blood had run over his left eye and dried to form a thick crust along the side of his face.

He scanned his surroundings, his swollen eye throbbing ceaselessly. From what he could make out, it appeared he was held captive in a building that resembled that of a chop shop. It wasn't very big but it was crammed with half-built vintage cars along with several untidy heaps of car parts. Above his head, a number of chunky chains hung from the thick steel rafters. There was no one else there, apart from the two large guys who were seated at a small square table in the far opposite corner—they were playing cards, oblivious to the fact that he was now watching them.

He suddenly recalled that he had slipped the envelope inside his jacket, so he looked down to see if his jacket had been opened. It hadn't. To be certain he gently moved his torso from side to side and heard the paper rustle against the inside of his jacket's zipper. He shut his eyes with relief. He'd have to somehow ensure it stayed undetected. No good would come from it if Wu found the envelope. It would just exacerbate the treacherous position he now found himself in—once again.

A burst of hope flooded his mind as he suddenly recalled the earpiece and hidden microphone. With any luck, it might still be there. Luck. It hadn't served him well lately. Perhaps Adam was right. Perhaps there was no such thing as luck.

With his hands securely tied behind his back, he opted to lower his ear onto his shoulder, making sure his movements were as unnoticeable as possible. But much to his disappointment, the earpiece was gone. He concluded that it must have fallen out during the struggle. He quickly moved on to assess if the hidden microphone was still connected. He flexed his torso and carefully moved to feel if the microphone was still stuck against his skin. But from under the weight of the armored vest, he couldn't be certain. If there was a chance that they could hear him, he needed to take it. If not, then all that remained was the hidden camera in the button on the left lapel of his jacket. He dropped his chin to his chest and looked to see if it was still intact. It was. But there was no way to know for certain if it transmitted. All he could do was try to communicate with Gabriel and hope for the best.

When he looked up, the two men were still seated in the same position. Again he dropped his chin to his chest and whispered down the opening in his jacket.

"If you can hear me, I'm fine. I lost the earpiece. Not sure where I am but I was taken by Wu. I have two guys watching me and I'm tied—"

"Hey! Who are you talking to?" one of the watchmen suddenly yelled out at him.

Lenny didn't answer.

"Don't even think about trying anything. We have orders to kill you if you try to escape!"

"Then why am I here if you plan to kill me anyway, huh? What do you want from me?" Lenny replied with bravado—also hoping that the microphone was transmitting.

"Shut up! The boss will deal with you when he gets here."

Lenny held back his words. There was no point in infuriating them. He couldn't risk having them find the hidden devices. He'd wait it out. And try praying.

NEARLY TWENTY MINUTES HAD PASSED SINCE GABRIEL first sent out the tactical team. Adam had been waiting patiently in his car.

"What's taking them so long?" he asked.

"They're en route, Adam. A bus collided with a taxi and the traffic is backed up. They've taken an alternative route. Stay put."

"Copy that."

But Adam's words had barely left his lips when he spotted Wu and The Midget pull into the parking spot two spaces ahead of him. He ducked down between the seats. *Please don't let them find me.* His heart pounded hard against his chest before the thumping settled at his temples. If he was able to see which building they entered he'd know where to tell the team to find Lenny. He slowly raised his head just above the dashboard. Wu and his henchman had crossed the road where they now stood in front of a large steel door painted with obscene graffiti. The Midget turned around and scanned up and down the street—clearly careful not to be seen. Adam ducked again, pinched his eyes shut, and hoped he'd done it quick enough. He moved to lock his car, just in case. But when a few minutes later he thankfully remained undetected, he sat up again slowly and stared at the graffitied door.

A sudden sense of urgency welled up within him. If Wu and his giant sidekick were on site, he'd certainly make good on his promise to let Jerome finally have his way with Lenny. He couldn't let that happen. Why else would they have taken him captive if not to teach him a lesson—or kill him.

With the tactical team still nowhere to be seen, Adam hopped out of his car and swiftly crossed the road. When he reached the steel door he placed his ear against it. There was no sound coming from inside the building.

"Gabriel, I'm going in. I can't wait. Lenny might be dead by the time your team arrives."

"Negative, Adam! Abort! I repeat, wait for tactical."

But Adam had already opened the door and entered the building.

ONCE INSIDE HE HELD BACK JUST INSIDE THE DOOR TO take in the premises. To his left, there was a large industrial staircase that led to a small office space. To his right was a hoist on which roller chains operated the rusty manual garage door he'd seen from the outside. Directly in front of him, several large metal drums were stacked on top of each other which obscured his view into the building. Using the drum wall as cover he slowly popped his head around one end. Lenny sat tethered to a chair in and amongst what looked like chopped up vehicles and car parts. Lenny's back was towards Adam and his head was dropped forward onto his chest. It looked as if he'd just taken a beating from Jerome who stood tall and belligerent in front of him.

In the distance, Adam heard male voices. They were laughing. When Jerome briefly turned his back on Lenny, Adam took his opportunity and bolted across the floor, ducking in behind one of the unfinished cars. His heart beat rapidly in his ears. Adrenaline rushed through his limbs. Needing to take a moment to steady his heartbeat, he fell back against one of the car's wheels. *Help us get out of here, please, Lord. Give me the courage to face them.* In a desperate attempt to rid his tight stomach of the tension, he took a deep breath in then exhaled slowly. It didn't help.

The men laughed again as if they were watching something hilarious. He steadied his wobbly legs. Hunched over he took a look through the car's windows. In the far corner of the warehouse, Adam spotted Wu seated next to two more of his men. He heard the thud of Jerome's fist hitting Lenny's face. It made him sick to his stomach to realize that was what Wu and his men were laughing at.

In his ear, he heard a scratchy noise and ducked back down against the wheel. He pushed the earpiece deeper into his ear, then checked the small radio transmission box that was hidden beneath his shirt. For a split second, he heard Gabriel's voice trying to break through the static but the signal dropped. There was now no way of knowing if the tactical team had arrived.

As the sickening sounds of another beating echoed through the space, Adam could no longer refrain from doing something. He had to come up with a plan, and quickly. *Distraction!* His eyes frantically searched the space around him. About ten feet away, in front of the nose of the car, a wheel wrench shaped like a cross lay on the floor next to three old tires. If he could throw that in the opposite corner of the unit it would certainly cause the men to leave their posts—and hopefully Jerome too. But getting to it put Adam at risk of being seen. He crawled along the car and stopped in line with its front fender. As he prepared to make his move, his muscles flexed and ready to charge, he heard the entrance door open then slam shut behind him. With not many places to hide, he quietly slipped into the car and lay down behind the front seats.

Several footsteps passed by him. For a long second his heart stopped beating altogether. With his breath lodged in his lungs, he remained in hiding. Waiting. Praying. When the footsteps were a fair distance away, Adam moved for the first time. From inside the car, he peered out the window. Jerome was no longer torturing Lenny—that was a relief.

In the far corner where Wu had sat laughing with his men, Adam had an obstructed view of a few more guys who'd joined him. They were talking, their backs toward Adam. He couldn't make out any of their conversation but the serious tone it held made the hairs on the back of his neck stand up. There was something familiar about one of them. As if he'd heard the man's voice before. He fell back behind the seats and searched the chambers of his mind.

And then it struck him, like a brick that got lobbed at him and hit him between his eyes.

The voice belonged to the one person none of them would have ever expected to be there. A man as deceitful as the devil himself. It was Diaz.

CHAPTER TWENTY-FOUR

Relieved that The Midget's ceaseless beatings had been interrupted, Lenny spat a glob of bloody saliva onto the floor in front of his feet. His mouth was numb and inflamed—as if he'd just returned from having all his teeth pulled at the dentist. His already swollen eye was now completely closed up. Having to now rely on the vision from his other eye proved a challenge too—it had taken a massive pounding under Jerome's enormous fists. For a brief moment, he allowed himself a sense of satisfaction as he recalled The Midget's face when he tried to punch him in the stomach and his fist hit Lenny's armored vest underneath his jacket. Without it, he'd probably have been dead already. His jaw ached too. A lot. For a moment he thought it might be broken. But when he managed to move it sideways, he was once again relieved. Perhaps he deserved this beating—for all the sins he'd committed in his life. For getting his innocent sister dragged into this mess. For ignoring God. Maybe this was the price he needed to pay. But maybe, just maybe, if he asked nicely, God would not be picky and forgive him.

Barely conscious of the world around him the rumblings between Wu and his men broke through the turmoil in his mind. They were talking about a hot deal. Then Wu mentioned five million dollars. Suddenly another man spoke. He said ten million. *They're negotiating.* Lenny used what little strength he had left in his body and lifted his head, skewed it sideways so he could attempt to see the man's face with what vision remained in his good eye. But even his sideways glance didn't help much. His vision was blurry, too blurry to see properly, but the very little Lenny did manage to make out, was enough to tell him that the other man was Diaz.

His insides felt as if he'd just swallowed a heavy stone that now wedged inside his stomach. Soon that was replaced by an anger so fierce he thought he'd lunge forward and plow into the man—chair and all. But he restrained himself. Listened. Watched as they shook hands. *Two-faced traitor!*

But worse than being double-crossed by Diaz was the knowledge that he most definitely didn't need Lenny's package anymore. And what that meant, in turn, was that Lenny had lost any hope of saving his sister.

The thought had him suddenly eject what little content he might have had in his stomach. So quickly did it catch him off guard that it landed in his lap. The involuntary purging sounds attracted unwanted attention from his nemesis and he cursed himself for letting them see how weak he was.

But his pride was soon forgotten when he watched as Wu and his minions left without so much as a glance his way. And moments after, Diaz's expensive leather shoes sounded on the floor towards him.

WHEN WU AND HIS MEN MOVED PAST ADAM WHERE HE was still in hiding inside the car, Adam once again held his breath, praying they wouldn't find him. When the door slammed shut he popped up intending to rush to free Lenny. But as his head rose above the doorframe, he spotted Diaz on his haunches in front of Lenny.

The unexpected turn of events forced him to think quickly. Diaz was on his own. Perhaps, between Lenny and himself, they could take him down. But if Diaz was armed it could get Lenny killed before he even got close. Deciding he needed to at least try to get within better reach, he sneaked out of the car—careful not to make a noise. This time he hid at the rear. In the distance, he heard police sirens and wondered if the tactical team was finally arriving. But when it suddenly went silent, he dismissed the notion.

But he wasn't the only one who heard the sirens. Diaz had heard them too—and it spooked him.

The bone-chilling sound of a switchblade echoed through the space and seconds later Adam watched as Diaz's hand sliced through the zip cord around Lenny's feet before he did the same with his hands. Once again Diaz's actions surprised him.

"Get up!" Diaz yelled at Lenny.

Adam looked on as Lenny stumbled to his feet with the knife pointed at his chest. Diaz swung Lenny around and shoved him towards the exit. Again Adam thought of attacking Diaz from behind, but when they neared, he decided against it. Partly because he lost his nerve, but mostly because Diaz would hopefully lead him to Carrie.

Adam hung back and held his position behind the car. When he heard the exit door open he cautiously charged towards it. He counted to five before he slowly opened the door—just enough to see where they were headed. Diaz shoved Lenny into the trunk of a silvery blue sedan car that was parked not far from Adam's. When Diaz pulled away, Adam sprinted from the building and slipped in behind the wheel, his sights fixed firmly on the rear of Diaz's car. This time he wouldn't lose Lenny. His attention was fully directed to the task at hand.

With his hands gripped firmly around the steering wheel, his knuckles white, he followed them.

At one of the junctions, the traffic light turned red just after Diaz crossed, and before he could. He ignored it and instead flattened his foot on the accelerator, narrowly missing several oncoming vehicles. With mere seconds to spare he spotted Diaz rounding the corner. As he turned the corner behind them he realized Diaz was heading toward the freeway. *Where's he taking him?* Once they hit the expressway, Diaz settled at a comfortable speed and Adam followed suit—maintaining his position at least three cars behind. Twenty minutes into the trip the gas warning light flickered on his dashboard. Adam's stomach tensed up and he eased his foot off the gas pedal. He'd have at maximum forty miles left in his tank before he ran out. At that speed, most likely even less. So he did what he always did lately when he needed to stand firmer in faith. He declared God's word out loud. Standing in faith that by God's divine power he wouldn't run out of gas.

And as he confessed the Word out loud, Gabriel's voice suddenly sounded in his ear.

"Adam, can you hear me? Are you okay?"

"Yes, yes, I can. Can you hear me?"

"Loud and clear my friend. I thought we'd lost you. Where are you?"

"I lost all communication with you. The signal died or something, but I'm okay. The Midget had a feast with

Lenny, knocked him around pretty badly. But he's holding up. Wu did some kind of deal with Diaz and Diaz took Lenny. I'm following them on the I-20 east-bound, about thirty-five miles outside the city. I'm low on gas though."

"Okay, stay on them. I'll get a bird in the sky. And, Adam, this time please wait for backup."

"I'll try, but I think he might be taking Lenny to wherever he's been keeping Carrie hostage. Wait! He's turning off. It looks like a—"

The crackling noise in Adam's earpiece returned.

"Gabriel? Hello, can you hear me?"

But Gabriel didn't respond.

The signal had dropped again. Perhaps he was too far out of range. Or perhaps it was because he was in the middle of nowhere.

Adam turned his attention back to Diaz's car ahead of him. As he took the turnoff onto a dirt road, he temporarily lost sight of their car in the dust clouds that kicked up behind it. The road stretched out between large open spaces on both sides. But as far as he could tell there were no roads that branched off.

It would be dark soon and his lights would give away his position. He searched for the switch on his dashboard to turn the auto-detection off. In the brief second it took to find it he was caught by surprise when Diaz's rear brake lights suddenly beamed through the cloud of dust in front of him.

He slammed both feet on his brakes, nearly sliding off the road as his car's wheel slid over the loose gravel. Caught in a giant cloud of dust the car jolted to a halt.

When Adam finally breathed again, and the cloud settled, he noticed Diaz had parked his car about a hundred fifty yards ahead. Thankful he had disengaged the auto light switch in the nick of time he slowly rolled his car off onto the side of the informal road and turned the engine off. As he took in his surroundings he noticed it was a large construction site—or something resembling a quarry. In the dusk light, he just about managed to see Diaz force Lenny out of his car's trunk. This time he had replaced the knife with a gun.

Adam cringed. He despised weapons of any kind. He tried reaching Gabriel, but the transmission was still down.

From a distance, still seated inside his car, he watched as Diaz shoved Lenny toward a mobile site office. There were no lights on inside. Both disappeared into the office. Less than a minute later, Diaz came out on his own. He lingered at the door after closing it, then made his way back to his car. The thought that Diaz would be heading back toward him suddenly dawned on Adam—he'd see him without any doubt.

Adam turned his car's ignition on but his car wouldn't start. His heart skipped several beats as he tried it again. His car was dead. His eyes remained pinned on Diaz's car where he was backing up to turn it around. *Come on! Start!* But still, his car didn't start. He needed to get out of there and fast or Diaz would drive straight into him. With nowhere to hide and no safe means of getting away fast enough, Adam flung his door open and ran as fast as his legs would allow.

In the distance behind him, he heard Diaz's car engine roaring up the road. He looked back, only for a split second. But it was enough to have his foot hit an uneven patch of dirt. He slammed down flat on his stomach, his face planted firmly into the hard ground. For an instant, he lost his wind and gasped for air. While he struggled to get to his feet he heard the engine close behind him. He saw the vehicle's lights beam alongside him and realized Diaz had no intentions of stopping.

CHAPTER TWENTY-FIVE

L enny groaned when his tortured body hit the rough carpet where Diaz had shoved him onto the floor. It was pitch dark inside the office. So much so that he couldn't see anything in front of his face. Or might it be because his eyes were swollen shut?

Diaz had bound his wrists together with duct tape, wrapping it extra tight because of the cast on his arm. At least they weren't behind his back this time. He wiped away at the beads of sweat that had trickled down his face, causing his vision to blur even more. But another wipe with the back of his hand did the trick and he could make out the faint outlines of a desk and one or two pieces of office furniture.

In the poor light, he managed to see the single window in the wall opposite him. On the outside it had timber nailed across nearly the entire pane, allowing the last bit of the day's light to filter through the narrow openings between the boards. The cold air it let in through the gaps had him brace himself for a cold night.

He knew he had to do whatever it took to try and break out, but he just couldn't seem to peel his exhausted body off the floor. Truth be told, he could have let himself fall asleep right there and never wake up, but he chose to force himself into a seated position. As he sat there wallowing in self pity, he thought he heard something move in the corner nearest to the window opposite him. With one half-open eye, he peered into the darkness. A portion of the desk obstructed his view, so he didn't care to look any further —he was too tired to move. But as he dropped his head back against the wood-paneled wall behind him, he heard the shuffle again.

At first, he thought it was a rat, but then realized it was too loud to be a rodent. Even one of the big ones. Whatever it was, he didn't want to chance it. Chills ran down his spine and the thought of sharing a space with any kind of critter creeped him out. Deciding he'd rather lie down on top of the desk—just in case—he pushed his body up from the floor and got into an upright position, momentarily losing his balance as he did so. When he moved toward the desk that stood in the centre of the room the shuffle sounded again. This time the shuffling was much more intense. But even standing up he couldn't see into the dark corner. The thought crossed his mind that perhaps this was some kind of holding cell for everyone who antagonized Diaz. A place he left his enemies to die. Why wouldn't he? He was useless to Diaz. And no one would even miss him.

Deciding he'd bravely face whatever it was so he could get some sleep, he moved around the desk towards the dark corner. A faint human whimper stopped him dead in his tracks. He could have sworn it sounded female. *Could it be?*

"Carrie?" he asked in a timid voice.

"Carrie, is that you?"

"Leonard?" Carrie's weak voice answered.

"Yes, it's me, you're alive!"

In one large step, Lenny leaped toward the dark corner and dropped to his knees. She was frozen stiff where he found her curled up in the corner.

"I've got you, sis, hold on. I've got you."

"Leonard, you came for me."

"Of course I did. I'm so sorry I got you into this mess. I am so sorry."

And for the minutes that followed they huddled together, quietly crying in each other's arms for the first time in almost a decade; leaning against each other just like they had all those years ago when their father beat their mother senseless.

Once they'd both grieved the time they'd been apart, reaffirmed their sibling bond, and silently exchanged forgiveness, it was Lenny who spoke first.

"We need to get out of here. Who knows what he'll do to us when he gets back."

"It's useless. I've tried. I found some train tracks not far from here, but somehow he caught up with me. They nailed the window and door shut. I think I heard the timber break away from the door when they put you in here. But I can't be sure. There's no way out."

"There's always a way out, little sister."

Lenny got to his feet and walked over to the window. Shards of glass crunched beneath his feet. He dropped down to his knees and smoothed his hands across the floor, feeling for a piece large enough to reach the tape around his wrists. The edges of the glass were sharp and it didn't take long before his hands were free.

"Are you tied up too?"

"Yes, but they used cable ties. My hands and my feet. It hurts, Lenny," she sobbed now.

"I know, I know. Just hold, on sis."

Taking the piece of glass with him he felt his way in the dark around her bound wrists. When he applied pressure he felt the sharp sting at the soft flesh between his thumb and index finger as the piece of broken window sliced through it. But he hardly cared. All he cared about was freeing Carrie. Once more he pushed down hard onto the piece of glass and the cable tie snapped apart. Carrie let out a soft moan when the plastic that had sliced into her flesh pulled away some of her skin.

"Sorry," Lenny empathized.

The ties around her ankles took a little longer—and left the cuts in his hands a little deeper. But his mind had numbed his body to the pain.

"Stay down for now until I find a way out of here. Just rest a bit," he told her.

But she was right. The timbers across the broken window were firmly in place and not even several hard knocks with his shoulder made any difference. He moved across to the door. That too had been secured with what sounded like a chain. But if there was one thing Lenny did well then it was to persevere. It was what had gotten him through his miserable life—never giving up when his back was against the wall. But no matter how hard he tried, or which corner of the office he searched in, there was no way out.

And as he walked back toward his sister and knelt down beside her to see if she was okay, he briefly caught himself asking God to help them. He'd never prayed before and there was no way he knew if he even did it the right way, but, at that moment, he hoped the God Adam spoke of heard him.

Exhausted from the torture his body had gone through, from all the years of running and hiding, he sat on the floor next to Carrie. She felt the blood on his hands and wiped it with the sleeve of her coat. And the thought crossed his mind, that even if they both died there, sitting on the floor next to each other, he'd leave this wretched world with the peace of knowing he had reconciled with his sister. If there was a God that heard him, if he was as dependable as Adam had said, and if he could find a way to help them, he would let him.

The thought was somehow freeing and he sat there in silent reflection, allowing it to wash over him.

When he leaned his head back against the wall, and opened his eyes again for the first time since he let it all go, he spotted it. At that precise moment, a cloud had shifted just enough to allow the tiniest beam of moonlight to break through a crevice between the timbers on the window, and it hit a section on the ceiling directly above the desk.

There, concealed to blend with the wood veneer panels in the ceiling, was a small square hatch.

It took all of three fleeting seconds for Lenny to jump up and onto the desk. Where he had managed to find the energy from he didn't quite know, but with almost no effort at all, he smashed his casted fist through the wood panel. It splintered easily to reveal the small cavity beneath the steel roof. Again he punched at the roof with his broken arm. He flinched as bolts of pain shot up through his bones. But freedom was in sight and that was all he could think of now. It took several more thrusts, before the corrugated steel sheet peeled away and Lenny stared up into the dark blue night sky.

And as he stared up at the heavens above, a little voice deep down in his soul told him God had heard his humble prayer.

"You did it, Leonard, you did it," Carrie said, her voice heavy with emotion.

"Time to get out of here." He smiled down to where she stood by his feet.

Once she had safely made it up and through the hole, he followed. With part of the flat roof damaged they needed to tread with caution. But when they got to the edge and saw how high they were off the ground, they nearly lost all hope again.

As Lenny stared out into the darkness across the open terrain, one eye still swollen tight, he saw the headlights of a car swerving and speeding across the landscape. For a few moments, he considered that it might be a group of guys having fun during a reckless binge. But when Carrie confirmed the color of the car appeared to be silver, he suspected that it was Diaz.

There was no time to spare. They needed to get down and run as fast as they could. While keeping a watchful eye on Diaz's location, Lenny positioned one of the roof panels down the side of the office. The ramp wasn't very stable but it was all they had to work with.

It did.

As soon as their feet hit the ground they ran in the

direction of the train tracks, hoping, praying Diaz wouldn't see them.

But when they were in close proximity to where Diaz was performing a donut maneuver like a crazed teenager, they heard the unmistakable cries of Adam's voice.

CHAPTER TWENTY-SIX

Adam ducked as Diaz swerved his car toward him once again. Dust clouds obscured his vision and settled in his eyes. He tried to run, but Diaz blocked him off, narrowly missing his legs. The harder Adam pushed to escape, the more fun Diaz had in torturing him. Even over the loud roar of his vehicle's engine, Adam could hear Diaz's crazed laugh billowing from his car's windows.

"What do you want?" Adam shouted at him, his voice raspy from the dust.

But Diaz wasn't going to answer. No matter how many times Adam shouted at him, begged him to let him go. Diaz had every intention of extending the sick cat and mouse game for as long as he deemed fit. Again he rammed his car forward. Then braked. Then thrust ahead toward Adam's legs. Braked again. Each time soliciting the precise response he'd hoped to get from Adam.

Diaz pushed forward once more. This time Adam held his position and didn't move. The unexpected defiance took Diaz by surprise and he came to a grinding halt inches away from Adam's legs. As Adam slammed both his hands flat onto the hood, he stared into his opponent's eyes.

Waiting for Adam to react, a sadistic laugh escaped from Diaz's lips and he revved his car to scare him off. But Adam stood firm. Instead, he told Diaz that he had a choice. That he could choose not to be this man whose heart was filled with hatred. That he knew the secret to making it all go away.

But Diaz ignored him.

With the car's nose aimed directly at Adam, its headlights illuminating the area around him, Adam stared his enemy full in his face. Like a matador staring out his bull, he stood his ground. Diaz revved his engine again. As if he was preparing to charge and lay the final sentence on his victim.

In the distance, a loud thundering sound distracted Adam and his head automatically turned to find the source. Diaz had done the same. The loud metallic noise rumbled towards them. It came from the mobile site office. And suddenly Diaz found himself torn between his two evil plans. He had left Lenny and Carrie inside the trailer with every intention of having them both die a slow and nasty death. And he had hoped to play his sick game with Adam until he finally had the urge to run him over.

Through the windshield, Adam now saw Diaz's eyes, darting back and forth between him and the noise at the office. The weight of having to make a choice was evident. When Diaz once again looked away, Adam took his chance and ran past the side of the car and off into the darkness. The difficult angle was enough to sway Diaz from chasing after Adam and instead he turned his car back towards the site office. As Adam turned around to look at Diaz, the car's headlights shone directly onto the trailer. Stationed next to the trailer Adam watched as Lenny and Carrie banged against a corrugated metal sheet. Their plan to distract Diaz from chasing after him—saving his life—had worked. Like a zookeeper who baited a predator away from his prey, they kept banging on the tin roof panel.

Diaz charged towards them, his heart filled with anger. His eyes stern and burdened with hatred.

"Get out of the way, Carrie!" Lenny warned.

The lights sped towards them.

The engine roared louder.

Diaz pushed the car faster.

With seconds to spare, Lenny shoved Carrie out of its path and lunged off to the other side. He hit the ground hard as the car sped past between them. Clouds of dust exploded into the space behind the car as Diaz ground to a halt.

"Carrie!"

"I'm fine!"

"Let's go!"

They scrambled to their feet and ran. As far as they could before Diaz could turn the car around and come for them again.

And he did. Quicker than they'd hoped he would.

But they didn't stop.

They heard the car's wheels spinning on the loose dirt.

Heard the stones kick up against the metal sheet.

Listened as Diaz pushed the car toward them.

From the corner of his eye, Lenny spotted movement in the dark.

Carrie fell, too weak to run further.

"Get up, sis, get up!"

He helped her up, watching as Diaz increased speed, closing the gap between them.

"Get in!" Adam suddenly yelled as his car screeched to a stop next to them.

He flung the passenger door open and yelled for them once more.

Carrie leaped into the front, Lenny in the back.

With their doors barely closed Adam flattened the gas pedal and maneuvered the car to kick up a curtain of dirt.

His car flew across the open space toward the road. In his rearview mirror, he looked out for the headlights that would come from Diaz's car. Moments later they came into view through the dust cloud behind them.

Adam floored the car, willing it to go faster. Next to him, Carrie moaned where she'd hurt her ankle when she tripped.

"You okay?" Adam yelled over his shoulder to both of them.

"I'm fine," Carrie said.

"I'll live," Lenny said.

"This man's not giving up! He's still behind us. It's going to take a miracle to get rid of him," Adam said.

"Can you lose him?"

"I'm sure going to try."

But Diaz knew the road like the back of his hand. And he wasn't going to let his prey get away, not by a long shot.

His car raced up behind them. Clipped their rear fender.

The impact caused Adam's car to fishtail in a patch of soft sand. His hands furiously worked at the steering wheel to get the car back onto the road. Then Diaz hit them again.

"Faster, Adam!"

But the accelerator was already flush with the floor beneath his feet.

"Hold on!"

Adam swerved the car off the road and over into the rough landscape. Diaz flew past. He braked hard, almost flipping his car over.

Adam didn't stop. The car's wheels dipped in and out of shallow potholes across the uneven plain. Then one front wheel hit a low ridge. The impact nearly blew the tire.

"He's turned around! He's coming, Adam," Lenny yelled keeping his eyes on Diaz.

"There!" Carrie suddenly yelled. "That's the train tracks I found."

Adam veered the car off into that direction.

Diaz was closing in again.

"This man won't stop until he kills us all," Lenny commented.

Their car hit another uneven patch which sent them up into the air before the nose slammed down hard on the ground. It lifted Lenny off his seat and deposited him hard onto the floor behind the seats.

A second later a single gunshot shattered the window where Lenny had been sitting seconds before he was thrown to the floor.

"Get down!" Adam yelled at Carrie to take cover.

She screamed as she ducked beneath the dashboard.

Another bullet whistled through the air and hit the frame of the car. It clanked off the steel with a hollow sound.

Adam pushed the car over onto the train tracks. The

railway sleepers hit the wheels as the car found the tracks. Adam moved the vehicle over them until he found a smoother path, keeping the car steady.

In his mirror, he watched as Diaz hit the same ridge they had just moments before. His car slammed back down, lifting Diaz from his seat and crashing his head against the steering wheel. The car slowed down. As if it had suddenly lost power. But only for a moment before it jerked back into position and continued its course. This time, however, it seemed far more determined.

"We can't keep riding the tracks. We're going to have to find a way out of this place," Adam yelled over his shoulder to where Lenny still lay on the floor behind his seat.

Lenny climbed back onto the backseat and told Carrie to stay down. His eyes frantically searched for another way out.

"There's nothing but this endless track. It could go on for miles," he yelled.

"I think that's the least of our worries! There's a train coming straight at us!"

Carrie squealed in fear. She kept her head down on her knees.

Lenny looked out the rear window.

"That maniac is still hot on our tail too, Adam."

Adam didn't answer. His focus was on finding a

way to escape being crushed between a maniac and a train.

On either side of the tracks were rows and rows of trees—the space between each too narrow for the car to fit through.

They were trapped.

The train's whistle warned them to move off the track.

Its lights grew sharper, closer.

Neither Lenny or Carrie spoke a word. Their eyes were fixed on the train up ahead.

Adam's hands were so tightly gripped around the steering wheel that his white knuckles glowed like fire-flies in the dark.

Behind them, Diaz was closing in, fast.

Adam wondered if his desire to see them suffer had made Diaz crazy enough to push them into the oncoming train—even if it meant sacrificing his own life in the process. *He would. He totally would.*

"Adam, we're not going to make it. There's no way out." Lenny finally spoke his thoughts out loud.

Carrie broke into an anguished sob.

The train's whistle blasted long and hard through the chilly night air.

Yet, Adam remained on course. Earlier he'd asked God to protect them and he still held firm in his faith that he would. The way he had always done for his children. The way Job had done when Satan tempted him.

God never let him go. A lonely tear threatened to roll down Adam's cheek as he felt God's presence come over him. When he let go of the wheel, for one small second just to wipe the wetness from his eyes, the railway track forced the car's wheels off the sleepers.

CHAPTER TWENTY-SEVEN

In one unexpected moment, a mere twenty yards away from the oncoming train, Adam's car veered off between two trees that were spaced precisely far enough for the car to fit through.

The sides of the car scraped between the trees where the momentum deposited them on the other side of the trees and onto a tarmac road.

When the car's nose pushed through a small bush after which it met with a single lane road, Adam yanked the wheel hard left in a furious attempt to regain control. For a brief moment, two of the wheels spun in the air as the car left the ground but then dropped down to hug the road.

"Whoohoo!" Lenny yelled out, patting Adam on his back then leaning over the front seats to kiss his sister on the cheek.

"You did it, Adam! You're a genius," Lenny kept praising.

"That, my friend, was all God," Adam replied, still in reverent awe at what had just happened.

But their moment of celebration was short-lived.

As they sped along the winding road that ran adjacent to the tracks, Diaz's car appeared from between the rows of trees in the distance behind them.

"The psychopath made it too! I can't believe it!" Lenny's indignant voice announced.

"Perhaps God's not done with him yet," Carrie replied quietly.

Her words caught Lenny off guard. He had no idea she too knew God.

He watched as Adam shared a sideways smile with Carrie as if they knew a secret Lenny didn't. It made him feel like they belonged to a private club he wasn't a part of.

Adam focused his attention back on the road. It was hard to see the road in front of them—they had lost one of the headlights during the escape between the trees.

"You'd better push it, Adam, before he catches up to us," Lenny urged.

But Adam's mind was occupied elsewhere.

"Hey, Adam, you're not listening. Put your foot flat, bud. We can't afford to slow down now."

He wasn't. At least not intentionally.

"I'm going as fast as I can, Lenny."

"No, you're not. Your foot's not even flat on the gas pedal. What are you doing?"

Adam didn't answer, his eyes darting between the dashboard and Diaz's car behind them. There was a fair distance between them, but it wouldn't take him long to catch up.

Lenny mumbled something under his breath while his eyes were nervously glued to Diaz's car behind them.

Adam's back stiffened in his seat as he shuffled into an upright position. As if he was preparing for something unexpected.

As his body stretched out he felt the transmission radio's adhesive tape pull across his skin under his shirt. Subconsciously his hand moved over his shirt to adjust it. At that moment static scratched in his ear. He had forgotten about the earpiece.

"Adam! Adam, do you read me?" Gabriel's voice blasted into his earpiece.

"Gabriel! Yes, yes, I can hear you." He smiled broadly.

"At last! That means you must have come back into range. Where are you?"

"No idea, but I have Lenny and Carrie with me in the car. They're fine, but we have Diaz on our tail. We're somewhere on a single lane road that runs alongside a railway track. There's a pine forest on both sides. I think we're heading east. But—"

"But what?"

"Well, we still have that small issue of an empty gas tank. I'm not sure how much further we have until we run out."

The announcement made Lenny's body run cold with terror. He leaned forward over Adam's shoulder to inspect the gauge on the dashboard.

"You don't have gas. I can't believe we're out of gas. Oh great!" he slumped back into his seat. His voice annoyed and laced with sarcasm.

Adam didn't react.

"Okay, my team's on it. Hang on. They're tracking the signal to the radio box as we speak."

"Please hurry, Gabriel. I think we're about to run empty."

"Copy that, Adam. Sit tight."

After seeing how much ground Diaz had gained behind them, Adam applied a tiny amount of pressure to the gas pedal and the car gave its first sputter.

"Get ready to get out and run," Adam said calmly.

"You're kidding, right?"

"Afraid not. Carrie, how's your ankle? Think you can run?"

"I'll try."

The engine gave another few spits before it finally

died. In an attempt to try to escape Diaz in spite of that, Adam turned the lights off and freewheeled the vehicle off the road and as far between the trees as the turf would allow. Once the car had left the road completely, and they were a fair distance in among the trees, the car ground to a halt and Adam killed the lights.

"Get out, get out. We need to find someplace to hide before he catches up and sees the car. Hurry!"

But as soon as Carrie stepped out of the car and applied weight on her injured ankle she cringed in pain and nearly fell. Adam and Lenny flanked her sides, scooped her arms over their shoulders, and ran. Hearts pumping, their stomachs tense with fear, they dragged her across the leafy forest floor. In the quiet of the night, they heard the rubber from the wheels of Diaz's car squeak on the tarmac before it came to a sudden halt.

They heard his door open, then close behind him. Leaves and twigs cracked under his feet as he entered the silent forest behind them.

Adam's eyes scanned for a place to take shelter. There was nothing but rows and rows of loblolly pines.

"Adam, what's happening?" Gabriel spoke in his ear.

"On foot. Trees. Chased," Adam replied in a hushed tone using as few words as possible to avoid being detected by Diaz.

"Copy that. We're suspecting you're in the plantation east of the city. There should be a river as it slopes down and away from the road. If that sounds familiar double-tap the earpiece."

It was too dark for Adam to see clearly but from the way his body weight had shifted, he could tell they were indeed on a slight downward slope. So he double-tapped the earpiece as instructed.

"Copy that. Good. Keep going toward the river. Once you get there, run west along the river. There's an old timber mill. I'm sending a team to meet you there. Tap again if you heard me."

Adam tapped twice.

"Great. This will be over soon, Adam. Stay safe."

But that was easier said than done.

Less than half a minute later a single bullet whistled through the air and smashed into a tree trunk ten feet away from them.

"I'll hunt you down till the end of time! I warned you not to cross me, Lenny! You're going to pay if it's the last thing I do, you hear me!" Diaz's deranged voice echoed through the forest. "You're not going to get away from me!"

Another bullet hit the dry leaves somewhere behind them. The abrupt sound caught Carrie off guard and she crouched forward. In doing so she threw them all off balance and they nosedived forward, narrowly missing a tree stump in the ground.

Lenny was up on his feet first. Then Adam. As they

pulled Carrie up and over their shoulders again, Diaz had gained significant ground. So close was he that they could almost hear him breathing right behind them.

The ground had become steep as it sloped down to where they could now also hear the river. Beneath their feet, the fallen needles were slippery and made it hard to keep a sure footing. Above their heads, the tree canopy blocked out any light the moon might have provided to help them find their way. A blessing in disguise in this instance, they realized, when they heard Diaz thump down onto the ground—obviously tripping over the tree stump.

It gave them enough time to reach the river and turn up in the direction of the mill, hoping, praying Diaz didn't see them.

"Where are we going?" Lenny whispered, his voice drummed out by the flowing river.

"There's a team waiting for us at a timber mill up ahead."

But the ground was uneven and muddy which made it harder for them to move fast enough. Several times the incline had them slide off into the icy water, cringing each time the water splashed noisily. But it was the same splashing sound that alerted them to the fact that Diaz had indeed found their trail and wasn't far behind.

"You can run but you can't hide, you fools. Sooner or later I'll catch up to you and you know it!" Diaz yelled in an enraged fit after he had landed in the water again.

His voice cut through the now icy night as he hunted his victims down. Driven by all things evil—anger, hatred, perhaps past hurts—Diaz had been taken over by an enemy only the faithful could survive.

"There!" Adam whispered and pointed to a clearing only twenty yards away.

From where they were they had to head up a short hill to where the outline of the timber mill appeared amid the darkness. The task was arduous with having to help Carrie walk and it wasn't soon after that they heard Diaz right behind them.

Adam's eyes desperately searched for the tactical team. To no avail. Desperate for their aid he risked it and called out to Gabriel.

"We're here," he whispered into the mic.

"Copy that, Adam. The team isn't far. Take shelter and wait for them."

The rural sawmill wasn't very big. With nothing but a roof structure in and among piles of lumber, there weren't many places to hide.

Behind them, Diaz's heavy breathing carried up the hill through the thin air.

"Where's the team?" Lenny asked when they ducked down behind a pile of logs next to the sawmill.

"They're coming. We need to stay low until they get here."

Lenny didn't need to say it. All three of them were equally terrified. They took shelter behind the logs and waited in silence, their hearts pounding in their chests, their bodies trembling in fear.

It was the chilling sound of snapping twigs that alerted them that Diaz had found them.

CHAPTER TWENTY-EIGHT

Moments later Diaz was right beside them, his glistening silver gun aimed at them, his index finger firm on the trigger.

"I told you I'd find you," he teased, his mouth curled into a sadistic smile.

"Get up!" He bounced the tip of his gun up and down.

When Carrie stayed seated on the ground between Adam and Lenny he yelled, "You too!"

"She's hurt," Lenny explained.

"Spot the worry in my eye, you traitor. Now get her up!"

Adam and Lenny did as they were told, holding Carrie up between them.

"What do you want from us, Diaz?" Lenny asked.

"I want you to pay for crossing me."

"I don't have any money."

Diaz bellowed a laugh.

"With your life, you idiot! Thanks to you I've lost ten of my top clients. That's millions of dollars! After your backhand deal with Wu, they've lost all trust in me and my business. Do you have any idea how long and hard I've had to work to build my reputation? You think you can come along and destroy it?"

"I didn't betray you, Diaz. It wasn't my fault." Lenny said, intentionally trying to extend the conversation to delay Diaz until the tactical team got there.

"Yeah, you see, that's where you're wrong, you slime ball." Diaz stepped closer and poked the gun's nose in Lenny's face.

The threatening tactic had Lenny's stomach turn upside down with fear.

"The only one who crossed you was Wu," Lenny said, his poker face firm and mere inches away from the barrel of the gun. All the while his insides were gripped with terror. But his tactic had worked.

His words had taken Diaz by surprise. The evidence of which was written all over his face.

"Oh, you didn't know. Now isn't that interesting?"

Diaz poked the gun closer to Lenny's face, the barrel now touching the tip of his nose.

"What are you talking about?" he demanded, lips pressed together.

"Wu was the one who stole the package from me in

the first place. He was cutting *you* out of the deal, my friend. And when I tracked him down and backed him into a corner, he blackmailed us into deciphering the contents. Except we didn't. Adam here sent him off on a wild goose chase. You're the one who was stupid enough to fall for his plan. He tricked you into trading the real formula for me. But you were so blinded with rage that you didn't even realize that he had double-crossed you. This is all on you."

Diaz fell silent as he tried to piece it all together, his eyes as cold as the icy ground they stood on. He glanced at Adam.

"He's telling the truth," Adam confirmed.

Diaz moved the gun from Lenny's face. He stepped back a few paces, turned sideways, and placed the back of his armed hand over his mouth, his other hand on his hip.

"Let us go, Diaz. Your war isn't with us," Adam spoke in a gentle tone.

Diaz turned his back on them and paced two steps away. They thought the truth had persuaded him to let them go free, but it hadn't.

It had done precisely the opposite. It angered him even more.

In an instant, Diaz's mood changed. He swung around, his eyes dark and consumed with rage. He had found a new target.

He aimed the gun at Carrie.

The sudden change of target left both Adam and Lenny unsettled and on edge, their hearts racing with dread.

"Leave her out of this, Diaz. She's got nothing to do with this. This is between you and me," Lenny said, his voice low and full of emotion.

Diaz shook his head and sucked the back of his teeth.

"Can't do that."

"Yes, you can. You don't have to take your anger out on her," Lenny begged. He was suddenly reminded of his childhood when he'd spoken those exact words to his father during one of his blow-ups on his mother.

"I'm not. I'm taking my anger out on you."

His confession left Lenny without words.

"You know, they should've named you Losing Lenny. The way I see it you're a loser no matter how hard you try. In fact, I bet you were born a loser."

Lenny didn't comment. His heart was heavy, burdened with years of regret. Burdened because perhaps Diaz was right.

"He's not a loser, and neither are you," Adam spoke up.

Diaz gave a scornful laugh.

"Oh wait, this is where you start preaching to me, right? Well, save it. I'm not interested."

He waved the gun in Carrie's face.

"You! Start walking."

When Carrie tried and couldn't she fell to the ground.

"I can't," she sobbed.

Lenny bent down to console her.

"Leave her alone!" Diaz warned, his gun now pointed at Lenny.

"Not today, *Losing Lenny*. Today is the day I'm going to take away the one thing that's most valuable to you—her! Then you can feel what it's like to lose everything you have."

Carrie sobbed harder as Diaz turned the gun back onto her.

His finger squeezed the trigger.

A shot fired.

"No!"

The sound of a bullet hitting its target rang in the air.

A second gunshot rang out, then a third.

Adam watched as Diaz dropped to his knees and slumped face-first to the ground.

From between the trees behind him, a tactical officer moved closer, his rifle up against his shoulder.

Adam knelt beside where Lenny had fallen on top of Carrie, his body folded over her when he took the bullet in his back and saved her.

Carrie let out a soft whimper.

"You okay?" Adam asked as he tried lifting Lenny's limp body off his sister.

She nodded.

When he was sure, he flipped Lenny over and onto her lap. With near-frozen hands, Adam moved to Lenny's neck, his fingers shaking, his chest tight with dread.

"Lenny?" Carrie cried next to his ear. "Lenny, wake up. Please wake up." She broke down. Her tears freely running onto her brother's bruised face.

But Lenny didn't move.

As the tactical team closed in on where Diaz lay wounded on the ground, Carrie stroked Lenny's cheek where his head lay in her lap. Her tear-filled eyes desperately searched Adam's face for answers.

Unable to give her what she was so desperate to find, Adam lowered his head to his chest and closed his eyes to seek his own answers.

And in the stillness of the night, between the tall loblolly pines, Lenny sucked in one sharp breath soon followed by two more.

As the oxygen filled his lungs, and his body recovered from the impact caused by the bullet that was blocked by his armored vest, Lenny finally found what he'd been looking for.

It was that very moment that Lenny realized; God had been at work in his life the whole time.

That nothing happened by coincidence and that luck had nothing to do with it.

And it had all come to this moment. The moment where Lenny realized that every good plan he'd ever made and failed at, had come together perfectly. Exactly as God intended it from the very beginning.

"For I know the plans I have for you," declares the Lord,
"plans to prosper you and not to harm you, plans to give you hope and a future"
Jeremiah 29:11

BOOK 3 - WHEN ADAM SAVES A HURRICANE SURVIVOR who washed ashore, his good deed lands him knee-deep in a global conspiracy that puts him and thousands in harm's way. Relying on his unique codebreaking skills, Adam wastes no time to untangle the dangerous web of terror that surrounds him. Good and evil are locked in an epic battle as Adam is left having to make a life-changing decision to save lives. But will it cost him losing his own?

EVERY GOOD WORK
(Book 3 in this series)

CHAPTER ONE

IT ONLY TOOK AN INSTANT TO REALIZE THAT HE WAS already dead when Patrick Phillips dropped to his knees next to the lifeless body of his client.

Dr. Bill Sutton's blank eyes stared into the space next to him, as though focused on something unseen. Fresh blood drenched the plush cream rug beneath his shoulders in his home office.

As if he wasn't convinced Bill was dead, Patrick leaned in to better inspect his face only to discover the horrific gash across his neck. He had never seen a dead body before, and it took every bit of inner strength to hold down the caviar he had enjoyed with Bill just a short while ago.

His heart pounded hard against his chest as his body now trembled with shock. Next to his knees, the pool of blood threatened to soak the designer suit he had specially bought for that evening's charity dinner. Jumping to his feet he stepped away from the body and stood anxiously staring at it with both hands clasped on top of his head.

In the background, he heard the dinner guests' chatter coming from the reception room at the end of the corridor. Suddenly aware that anyone could walk in on him at any moment, he panicked and rushed to close the door he had inadvertently left ajar. He needed time to think, time to make sure they wouldn't implicate him.

If caught alone in the room with the great Dr. Bill Sutton lying dead on the floor, it would take a lot more than his word to convince authorities he wasn't to blame. Why he felt such immense guilt over his death, he didn't know. Perhaps because deep down inside he had wished Bill dead a million times. To the world out there Dr. Bill Sutton was a saint, a savior of lives. But to him, Bill was the proverbial nightmare client no one wanted. The only reason he'd tolerated his condescending ways with him was because he was best friends with his son, William. And Bill had made it abundantly clear that his loyalty to his only son was the single reason he had agreed to let Patrick manage the company's financial portfolio. So they were each doing it for William. On that, they could agree. Everything else, not so much.

It was also no secret that Bill hadn't been pleased with his recent trading strategies. Patrick had lost him millions in a swing trade. He'd heard the rumors—Bill had been shopping around for a new portfolio manager. Without the Gencorp account, Patrick's company wouldn't even exist. Everyone knew that, and with Bill out of the way, William, his only son, and heir to Bill's entire fortune, would make void that threat.

That was motive.

He'd need solid evidence, an alibi.

And he had neither.

Patrick nervously circled Bill's dead body, careful not to step into the blood or leave any trace behind. With his palms now together over his nose and mouth, he took a deep breath to relax his shoulders and snapped the vertebrae in his neck back into place. He was used to thinking on his feet, deciding under pressure. Risk management was the very marrow in his bones.

With his eyes fixed on the dead body on the floor, his mind hurriedly worked through the dilemma. He was last seen flirting with Bill's attractive assistant before he made small talk with a few prospective clients. As far as anyone should be aware, he was still out there canvassing the room for new clients. Bill had joined a few of the other guests in the wine cellar. At least that's what Patrick had assumed when Bill had excused himself and walked off in that direction.

Patrick's mind worked through the events of the evening. If only he hadn't come looking for Bill. If only he hadn't felt so insecure over losing the Gencorp account and tried so hard to win back Bill's favor.

There was no doubt in his mind. He'd definitely be on the police's main suspect list. A list that wasn't that long. Bill didn't have enemies—he was far too good-natured for that.

The reflection triggered him to realize that his fingerprints were on the doorknob. He leaped across the room and, using his pocket square, wiped the handles on either side of the door. Pausing at the door, he readied himself to quietly sneak out but quickly let go of the notion when he heard footsteps approaching. Frazzled by the unexpected threat, his eyes searched for a place to hide as the footsteps grew closer. Moments before the doorknob turned to open the door, Patrick hid in a dark shadowy space between a floor-to-ceiling bookcase and a wall in one corner of the room. Unable to see the door, he stood there, shoulders squashed between the wall and the bookcase, his back stiff and his body on high alert. All he saw was Bill's unresponsive eyes staring directly at him. It made his stomach tense up; it was downright creepy, so he looked down at his feet instead. The door creaked open, then gently closed again. As he waited, barely breathing, he spotted a small oxblood leather notebook next to his feet on the floor. Intrigued, his eyes remained fixed on it while he listened for movement in the room. His instincts told him it had to have been the killer who had returned, and he guessed the book had something to do with it since Bill's eyes had fixed on it just before he died. If it were any of the guests, they'd have screamed by now.

He stood still, barely breathing as he listened. But the room was dead silent. It baffled him. What was he waiting for?

When, after a few moments, there was still no sign of anyone in the room, he slowly leaned forward and peered around the bookcase into the room. There was no one to be seen—at least not from his angle.

Perhaps the killer had left. Remaining cautious and alert, he bent to pick up the notebook. A shuffle to his right let him know he wasn't alone after all. It took a mere split second to be discovered by a man wearing a dark dinner suit and a black hooded mask with matching gloves.

Without another second to spare—for fear of being trapped in the corner—Patrick charged towards the door. But the masked figure was too quick, the silver blade of his knife glistening under the soft light of the overhead chandelier.

As quick as lightning, the killer's gloved hand thrust the knife forward and slashed across Patrick's arm. The sharp edge sliced through the sleeve of his suit and very nearly penetrated all the layers of his clothing. The motion had Patrick step back several paces, in the process nearly tripping over Bill's body.

"Who are you? What do you want?" Patrick yelled out.

The answer to one of his questions was obvious when, from behind the narrow slits in his hooded mask, the killer's beady eyes fixed on the leather notebook that was still clasped in Patrick's hand. With only Bill's body on the floor between them, there was little else to protect Patrick from ending up dead on the floor next to Bill.

"What's so important about this book that you'd kill a man over it, huh? Who are you?" Patrick asked again, hoping his questions would buy him some time until someone heard and came to his rescue.

The killer didn't answer. He'd seen through

Patrick's futile attempt to escape his wrath. Instead, a silent, slow dance of sorts ensued between them as they circled around Bill's body, the knife in the killer's outstretched hand hovering, threatening. Neither of them made the first move. Neither of them spoke.

As they turned once more, and Patrick faced the French doors that opened out onto a small veranda that overlooked the bay, he cast a swift glance at the light-weight curtain that stirred ever so slightly in the evening breeze. He couldn't be certain the doors were open, but if not, he'd break his way through the glass. If he could somehow be quick enough, he could escape across the lawn and disappear between the boats in the marina. It was his only option. Fleeing through the internal door and the house would give the killer the perfect opportunity to get away, leaving him the one who'd end up looking like the murderer fleeing the scene.

Preparing for his escape, he placed the notebook in the inside breast pocket of his jacket, his face arrogantly mocking the killer.

The killer remained silent.

"You know you won't get away with this. There are cameras all over this place. Your days are numbered, buddy," Patrick bluffed, attempting to distract the killer.

It worked.

Patrick watched as his beady eyes darted to the corners of the study. Using it to his advantage, Patrick gently manipulated their circular dance until he had his back facing the terrace doors.

"You're missing the one above the entrance door behind you," he deceived again.

When the killer turned to look over his shoulder, Patrick swung around and bolted for the French doors, pushing a chair down behind him as he passed it. His mind was laser sharp and focused on the slight parting in the middle of the two doors. With no effort, his lean frame and agility had him slip through the opening with ease.

Adrenaline pulsed through his veins as he took two long strides before he hoisted himself over the low wood railing to land feet first into the shrubs below. He lost his footing and rolled onto the expansive lawns but, thanks to his athletic prowess, was back on his feet and running in no time. Behind him, the killer's feet hit the deck. Patrick didn't turn to look for fear of losing his focus. He ran. As fast as his feet would carry him. Down the slight hill, towards the glistening lights in the small marina. Mere steps behind him, he heard the killer's strained breathing under his face covering.

He pushed his body harder, keeping his eyes on the marina some eighty yards or so away. It took several more strides, but he had gained enough distance between them. When he reached the bottom of the hill where the grass met with the white concrete walkway that led another thirty yards down into the marina, his eyes skimmed over the moored boats. There were at least fifty, ranging from large luxury yachts and catamarans to smaller sailboats. Spaced evenly along the now wooden walkway, the warm glow of overhead lamps illuminated every step he took. He'd need to get out of the light and hide—quickly.

Up ahead, positioned in the shadows between two lamps, he spotted a jetty leading off into the darkness between the boats. When he reached it, he quickly turned onto the floating jetty that ran between the two rows of large yachts. Hiding in one of the vessels wouldn't do. With only five of them on either side, it would be dead easy for the killer to find him. If he had any chance of escaping, he'd have to get into the water. Short on options, and short on time, he didn't hesitate.

When he reached the smaller landing stage between two enormous black yachts, he quickly stepped onto it, nearly losing his balance as the water moved beneath it.

Obscured by the large vessels, he retrieved the pocket-sized book from his jacket and secured it between his teeth.

Behind him, he heard the main jetty grind against the guide ropes as the killer's weight slowly moved over it toward him.

CONTINUE READING

GET YOUR FREE SUSPENSE THRILLER!

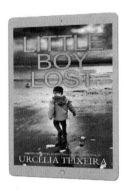

**A MISSING BOY. A TOWN BURIED IN
SECRETS. A DEPUTY WHO WON'T QUIT.**

https://home.urcelia.com

Beware the eye of the storm...

Adam Cross is left with a life-changing decision when he returns in the gripping
Christian suspense series finale!

When a massive hurricane hits Turtle Cove, Chief Perry and his team battle to
save the community. As the small coastal town's residents come together in the
wake of the disaster, the discovery of an unfamiliar survivor who washed ashore
has the townsfolk guessing.

But he isn't all the tides brought in.

Unable to recall his identity or the events leading up to him washing up on the
beach, mystery ensues, and it isn't long before the residents of Turtle Cove
realize there is something far more sinister in the making.

Something more fearful than the storm.

Full of mystery, twists, and turns, this last book in the best-selling Adam Cross series will grip you from the very first page and keep you reading until you reach the end!

READ MORE

(https://amzn.to/3ii6UyA)

DEAR READER

All glory be to the Lord, my God who breathed every word through me onto these pages.

*I have put my words in your mouth and
covered you with the shadow of My hand
Isaiah 51:16*

It is my sincere prayer that you not only enjoyed the story, but drew courage, inspiration, and hope from it, just as I did while writing it. Thank you sincerely, for reading *Every Good Plan*.

If you would like others to also be encouraged by this story, you can help them discover my book by leaving a review.
CLICK HERE

Writing without distractions is a never-ending challenge. With a house full of boys, there's never a dull moment (or a quiet one!)

So I close myself off and shut the world out by popping in my earphones.

Here's what I listened to while I wrote *Every Good Plan*:

- 10 Hours/God's Heart Instrumental Worship —Soaking in His presence (https://youtu.be/Yltj6VKX7kU)
- 2 Hours Non-Stop Worship Songs— Daughter of Zion (https://youtu.be/DKwcFiNe7xw)

When I finished writing the last sentence of the book! How great is our God—Chris Tomlin (https://youtu.be/KBD18rsVJHk)

AUTHOR CONNECT

STAY CONNECTED

Sign Up for Urcelia Teixeira's newsletter and get future new release updates, cover reveals, and exclusive sneak peeks and VIP reader discounts! (signup. urcelia.com)

FOLLOW ME

BookBub has a New Release Alert. Not only can you check out the latest deals, but you can also get an email when I release my next book, and see what I read and recommend. Follow me here

https://www.bookbub.com/authors/urcelia-teixeira

Website:

https://www.urcelia.com

Facebook:

https://www.facebook.com/urceliabooks

Twitter:

https//www.twitter.com/UrceliaTeixeira

VALLEY OF DEATH SUSPENSE THRILLERS

Toe-curling suspense thriller trilogy you won't want to put down once you start!

Readers say this is my best work yet!

Best enjoyed in sequence

VENGEANCE IS MINE - Book 1

SHADOW OF FEAR - Book 2

WAGES OF SIN - Book 3

ADAM CROSS SERIES- CHRISTIAN MYSTERY & SUSPENSE

Gripping faith-filled mystery and suspense novels laced with danger and adventure that

will leave you breathless on every page!

Also suited as standalone novels

EVERY GOOD GIFT - Book 1

EVERY GOOD PLAN - Book 2

EVERY GOOD WORK - Book 3

ALEX HUNT ADVENTURE THRILLERS

Fast-paced, clean archaeological adventure thrillers with a Christian worldview.
Inspired by actual historical events and artifacts
Also suited as standalone novels

Download the Free series prequel - download. urcelia.com

The PAPUA INCIDENT - Prequel *(not sold in stores) Free when you sign up*

The RHAPTA KEY

The GILDED TREASON

The ALPHA STRAIN

The DAUPHIN DECEPTION

The BARI BONES

The CAIAPHAS CODE

For more on the author and her books, please visit www.urcelia.com

Urcelia Teixeira writes gripping Christian mystery, thriller and suspense novels that will have you on the edge of your seat! Firm in her Christian faith, all her books are free from profanity and unnecessary sexually suggestive scenes.

She made her writing debut in December 2017, kicking off her newly discovered author journey with her fast-paced archaeological adventure thriller novels that readers have described as 'Indiana Jones meets Lara Croft with a twist of Bourne.'

But, five novels in, and nearly eighteen months later, she had a spiritual awakening, and she wrote the sixth and final book in her Alex Hunt Adventure Thriller series. She now fondly refers to The Caiaphas Code as her redemption book, her statement of faith.

And although this series has reached multiple Amazon Bestseller lists, she took the bold step of following her true calling and switched to writing what naturally flows from her heart and soul: Christian Suspense.

A committed Christian for nearly twenty years, she now lives by the following mantra:

"I used to be just a writer. Now, I am a writer with a purpose!"

For more on her and her books, please browse her website, www.urcelia.com or email her on books@urcelia.com

Never miss a new release!

Sign up to her Newsletter: signup.urcelia.com

Follow her on BookBub (https://www.bookbub.com/authors/urcelia-teixeira)

facebook.com/urceliabooks

twitter.com/UrceliaTeixeira

bookbub.com/authors/urcelia-teixeira

Made in the USA
Middletown, DE
12 October 2023